COLD FEET

JENNIFER YOUNGBLOOD

ARBOR
HOUSE

YOUR FREE BOOK AWAITS

Get Beastly Charm: A Contemporary retelling of beauty & the beast as a welcome gift when you sign up for my newsletter. You'll get information on my new releases, book recommendations, discounts, and other freebies.

Sign up at Jenniferyoungblood.com

WAKE UP AND FACE THE TRUTH

ou know that nightmare where you're back in high school and standing by your locker? You look down, horrified, to realize that you don't have a stitch of clothing on and everyone is staring? All you can think is, *Why did I eat that double-decker brownie piled with two scoops of ice cream last night? It went straight to my hips, and I have no way to hide it!*

Or the one where you're supposed to take a test in five minutes, but you haven't studied a lick for it? In fact, you didn't even remember that you were taking the class. Or how about the one where you're crossing the street and you can see a car coming from far away in the distance? You try to move, but your legs are heavier than a pregnant hippo, and you have concrete blocks welded to your feet.

Well, that's how I feel. The sad part is that it's not a dream, but my life. Five years ago, when I struck out for New York all starry-eyed and ready to take on the fashion world, I never imagined that I'd be back home in Comfort, Alabama, living with my parents. I'm single, jobless, and have the social life of a hermit. Pretty sad when the only thing I have to look forward to this weekend is binge-watching *The Bachelor*. I know. It's pathetic that I somehow find it entertaining to watch a gaggle of women trying to peck their way into one man's heart.

In my defense, I couldn't help it that the store I poured my heart and soul into for the past three years closed when investors decided to go a different direction. I had worked with my staff to increase the numbers, and we did—through much blood, sweat, tears, and a multitude of sidewalk sales. In the end, all our hard work went down the drain because some suits sitting around a polished boardroom table decided to put their resources into another box-store and go with the stack-it-high-and-sell-it-cheap mentality. Maybe I shouldn't have caved and let Mom talk me into coming home. She caught me at a low moment when my landlord was busting my chops about being late on my portion of the rent. Also, I had just gone into the kitchen to make myself a sandwich and was grossed out by the mountain of dirty dishes piled in the sink. My former roommate Mitzi would rather have a root canal than wash a dish. Normally, it wasn't too much of a problem because Mitzi was a runway model who never ate more than the few morsels required to keep her alive. However, Mitzi had just gotten passed over for an audition and chose to drown her sorrow by making pasta primavera ... three days prior! The dried sauce was so crusty that it looked like the dishes were covered in scabs.

Mom happened to call, and I broke down, bawling like a baby, telling her that my life was in ruins.

"Come home," Mom soothed. "You can regroup and make a plan."

What can I say? I'm a wimp. I caved.

Now, I realize the gravity of my error. I should've stuck it out in New York. I could've gotten a job at another clothing store working retail. Sure, it would've been tough to start at the bottom of the totem pole again, but at least I would've been in control of my life. Eventually, I could've found another management position. Why did I let my rotten circumstances get the best of me?

"Because the bed in my old apartment wasn't nearly as comfortable as this one," I murmur as I sink deeper into the covers and channel my mind into a pleasant dream that I float into like a bird taking refuge in a soft cloud—I'm walking on a beach in Hawaii. The sun, shining like a bright copper penny, feels so deliciously good on my face. The hunk striding toward me is shirtless, his bronze muscles shimmering almost as much as the silvery ocean. His eye catches mine as he smiles.

The next thing I know, the covers are being ripped from my body. "What's going on?" I shriek.

"Good morning," Mom chimes as she traipses over to the window and pulls back the drapes to let in a blinding splash of morning sun. "Time to get up."

Always one to come out swinging, indignant words fly from my mouth like razor-tipped arrows. "It's not time to get up! It's only ..." I contort my body around to the nightstand and fumble for my phone. "Eight-thirty," I mumble as my eyes bulge. Holy cow! Is it really eight-thirty? I can't remember the last time I've slept this long. I'm normally out of bed by seven at the latest. A merciless headache throbs across the bridge of my nose with the force of a prize boxer going for the winning knockout. I want to just close my eyes and block out the world. Instead, I sit up and rake the hair from my face. Maybe it wasn't such a good idea to gorge my blues with two fudge walnut brownies and a half-gallon of vanilla ice cream. No wonder I was having nightmares about being stark naked with thunder thighs. I must've gone into a sugar coma. Stringy bangs crowd my eyes, reminding me that I'm overdue for a haircut, a fact that my mom has been reminding me of since I got back into town.

"I'll set you up an appointment with Shelia or one of the other girls at the beauty salon," Mom has offered a dozen times.

Yeah right! Like I'm gonna go to the Curl Up or Dye Beauty Salon to get my hair done. No thanks. I'll come out looking like a Pomeranian poodle. I rub my eyes which are scratchier than sandpaper, trying to erase the cobwebs of sleep from my brain. The sight of Mom so cheerful and put-together makes my stomach churn. Mom is one of those people who's so perpetually happy that she's annoying.

While some women get their eyebrows tattooed on, I swear that Mom must've gotten her smile tattooed on because it hardly ever wavers. With her chestnut hair, almond-colored eyes, and petite build, people say that the two of us are dead-ringers. However, I've got a good five to seven extra pounds on me due to stress and, well ... life. Mom has managed to whittle away the extra pounds from her figure due to her regimented routine of yoga, the occasional visit to a plastic surgeon, oh, and the fact that she hasn't eaten a French fry since she was twelve.

If only I had a kernel of Mom's self-control, I'd probably be the CEO of a Fortune 500 Company instead of an out-of-work retail store manager. When Mom turned fifty-seven, she chopped off her shoulder-length hair so it wouldn't drag down her features but left it longer and fluffy on top. Her highlights are as fresh and perfect as her makeup. She's one of those quintessential Southern Belles who gets dressed up to go to the grocery store or even outside to check the mail.

A few months ago, right after Christmas, when a friend of Mom's passed away in a car accident, I happened to be home visiting for the holidays at the time and overheard Mom chatting with one of her friends who's a mutual member of the Lake Pines Women's Club. They were talking about how impressed they were with the funeral home that did Judy's makeup and decided that when they eventually kick the bucket, they would make sure that their loved ones enlist the services of said funeral home. Pretty typical of women in the South to put on a show to the very end.

Sadly for my mom, her only child, yours truly, did not fall in her footsteps of thinking that everything has to be perfect all of the time. Yes, I love fashion and design, but I'm not gonna flip my gourd if I have to go out of the house without makeup on occasion. I like to eat what I want and go casual in jeans and a t-shirt when the situation warrants. When I'm in a rut, I wanna sit around in my grubby clothes eating ice cream and watching Netflix. Is that such a crime? Sure, my hair needs trimming, but I'll get around to it ... eventually.

Mom's eyes are brimming with an excitement that makes me nervous. There is no telling what hare-brained scheme Mom has cooked up in her restless mind. Whenever I come home—even for a short visit—I become Mom's pet project. Now that I'm home for an interminable amount of time, things are bound to get hairy. Mom brings her hands together and launches in with, "So, are you ready to start your new life?" Her juicy voice reeks of over-ripeness.

"What do you mean?" I ask carefully as I moisten my lips.

"Do you remember how we talked about you doing alterations until you could find something more permanent?"

"Yeah." I study her through skeptical eyes. The alterations gig was Mom's idea. I went along with it because I didn't want to start off my stay at home by disagreeing with everything that she says. However, I'm not sure if I'm Kosher with the idea of doing alterations for the rest of my life. On the other hand, I could use the money. Even though I'm living at home, I want to feel like I'm making my own way. It would be humiliating to have to ask my parents to borrow a few bucks just so I can grab something to eat at a restaurant or purchase Ben and Jerry's ice cream.

"I've got your first client," Mom squeals.

I scrunch my nose. "Who?"

Hesitancy fills her expression. "Don't get upset."

It's amazing how fast those three little words get the blood pumping through my body. They are a red flag waving in front of a sleep-deprived, sugar-overloaded bull. "What did you do?"

She starts talking fast. "Did you know that Kitty Williams serves on the board with me at the Lake Pines Women's Club?"

No, I wasn't aware of that tidbit because I don't make a habit of keeping up with Mom's charitable organizations. She heads up several of them. It's her hobby, something to keep herself occupied while Dad runs his law firm. "Yes," I answer, figuring it's easier to just go along with it.

"Well, I happened to mention that you were coming back home, and Kitty said that Collette was looking for someone to alter her wedding dress." Mom's voice is high-pitched, and she's talking a mile a minute.

I don't have to be a genius to know where this was going. It's written all over Mom's face. My jaw hits the bed and ricochets back to my teeth as the air flies out of my lungs faster than the lead car at the

Daytona 500. "Collette's getting married?" The world begins to spin, and I wanna throw up. "To who?" I only thought I'd hit rock bottom when I left New York. From the sound of this, things are about to get a whole lot worse.

Mom's expression is both surprised and concerned. "I thought you said you were over Gavin."

"I am," I growl. "I was over him years ago." Traitorous tears threaten to pool in my eyes, but I win the battle and swallow them back down.

"That's right," Mom affirms. "You were head over heels with the doctor." She speaks the words with fervor, like she's trying to convince herself as much as me. I suspect that's because she feels the need to ease her conscience over getting me in such a pickle with Collette Williams. She pauses as if collecting her thoughts. "What was his name?"

"Who?" I squeak. It's hard to breathe, and my mind is swimming in a stagnant pool of unrealized expectations.

Mom looks at me funny. "The doctor." Her brows crease as she studies me with those perceptive eyes that have the power to unleash more of my secrets than the most sophisticated lie detector test ever could. "Are you okay? You're looking a little green around the gills."

"I'm fine," I assert, shooting her a death glare. "His name's Marshall," I thrust out through gritted teeth.

There was a brief period of time when I was enamored with Marshall Davis. I had thought that maybe the two of us might have a future together, until Marshall announced that he'd signed up as a volunteer physician in Ghana. The slot was initially supposed to be for six weeks. While I was disappointed that Marshall was leaving, I put on a brave face and told myself that it was only for a few weeks. Then, six weeks turned into several months until finally, I got an email—not a phone call, mind you—but a measly email from Marshall, telling me that he'd fallen in love with one of the nurses on his team. Oh, who cares about Marshal! His hair was always parted a little too straight for me anyway. He's one of those guys who's so busy saving the world that he's forgotten how to actually live. The sad truth is that Marshall was a placeholder for the only guy who's ever really claimed my heart. "So Gavin's marrying Collette." I have to say the words to make myself believe them. *Please let this be a bad dream.*

"Yes," Mom utters quietly before taking in a long breath. "I'm sorry, but I really did think you were over Gavin, or I wouldn't have volunteered you for the job." With the snap of imaginary fingers, her expression changes. "What's done is done, I suppose," Mom says pleasantly as she smoothes a hand over her cream-colored slacks. "I know you and Collette didn't get along all that well in high school, but it's time for you to start fresh."

Blood is rushing so profusely to my head that I wonder if it will pop off my neck and launch clear up to space. "No!" I nearly shout. "I'd rather be tarred and feathered before I work on a dress for Collette Williams." Collette and I were on the cheerleading squad in high school. While we'd never been close friends, we got along okay until I beat out Collette for the head cheerleader position. From that moment on, Collette hated my guts. I wouldn't put it past her to marry Gavin just to spite me. I had heard through the grapevine a few months ago that Collette and Gavin had gone on a date or two, but I didn't think it would go anywhere. I figured Gavin was too smart to get mixed up with a high-maintenance diva. Evidently, I was wrong.

Mom sits down beside me on the bed and places a hand over mine. Her voice is practical, determined as she squeezes. "Look, this is a good opportunity. It'll get your foot in the door. People listen to Kitty. A recommendation from her is as good as gold." Mom gives me a pleading look which only she can perfect. "Please? It would mean a great deal to me if you'd do this one, teensy thing."

I hate it when Mom goes all soft and contrite on me. While she prides herself on being an outstanding president of charitable organizations, she missed her calling. She should've been a hostage negotiator. Given enough time and persuasion, Mom has always been able to mold me, and every other person she has a mind to influence, like putty. I feel myself getting pinned into a corner with no hope of an escape. "Fine," I mutter. "I'll do the stupid alteration." I raise an eyebrow. "But it had better not be too involved."

"Fantastic!" Mom exults as she stands. "You'd better hurry. Collette and Kitty will be here at nine."

A hard laugh scratches my throat. "Of course they will be," I grumble. I had known from the minute Mom waltzed into my room that she had something up her sleeve. "I'm gonna get in the shower." *And I'm taking all the time I need*, I add mentally. "If Collette and Kitty get here before I'm done getting ready, they can just wait." I level a glare, daring Mom to disagree.

She frowns. "It's never a good idea to keep clients waiting."

Fighting the urge to scream, I point toward the door. "Just go."

"See you downstairs," Mom chimes as she hurriedly leaves the room.

My headache is now a thousand times worse. With every throb it feels like someone is taking a chisel to my brain. My stomach growls and I roll my eyes. Seriously? How can I possibly be hungry after last night's gorge session? My stomach had better get a grip because I certainly can't keep caving to its demands, or I'll need a new wardrobe before the month's end.

I can't believe that Gavin is getting married to Collette! The world has gone mad. A feeling of deep sadness washes over me, but I immediately tamp it down. Maybe this is a good thing. Gavin's moving on with his life. If he wants to marry Collette and be one of those Instagram husbands whose only ambition in life is to capture the perfect snapshot of his demanding wife, then so be it. Collette has deemed herself an influencer and has a smattering of a following. She's constantly doing hair and makeup tutorials. Not that I've paid much attention, mind you. I just happened to see a few of her posts.

Gavin, however, is a different story. I'm not proud to admit this, but in my weaker moments, I have resorted to stalking him on social media. Interesting that he hasn't put up any pictures of him and Collette, and his profile status is still listed as *single*. Trust me, I know because I checked it two days ago. It's not hard to see why Collette Williams is itching to get her claws into Gavin, but why is he settling for her? Gavin could have anyone he wants. *Too bad he doesn't want me*, my brain shouts.

Gavin has always been a chick magnet, even back in high school. As if his looks and charming personality weren't enough to seal the deal, he had the accolade of being a star athlete to boot. Now that he owns the local hardware store and a healthy share of rental property —both commercial and residential—his appeal is bound to shoot to the moon. An image of Gavin flashes through my mind. I've always loved the reckless vibe that Gavin's dark-brown, messy hair gives him. Add to that his arresting honey-green eyes, rugged features, and quick smile, and it's not hard to figure out why I've had a hard time getting over him. Gavin could always make me laugh. He taught me not to take myself too seriously. In short, I liked the person I was when I was with him.

This is ridiculous! I can't keep wallowing in self-pity. What did I expect? That I'd waltz back home and find Gavin waiting for me with open arms? That only happens in cheesy romance novels. This is no romance novel, and I'm certainly no heroine. I'm a washed-up fashionista wannabe with an over-zealous mother who couldn't stay out of my business if her life depended on it.

And now, like it or not, I'm about to alter the wedding dress of my high school archenemy who's engaged to my former boyfriend, my biggest regret—the itch I never could scratch, the one man who shattered my heart into a thousand pieces and then walked out of my life without so much as a parting glance.

"A fine morning this is turning out to be," I growl as I stalk toward the shower.

It's time for this girl to wake up and face the truth. Gavin has officially moved on. Now I need to do the same. The question is ... how?

GOOD GRIEF, IT'S ONLY A PINPRICK

When I slink down the steps, my hair still damp, I find Mom, Kitty, and Collette waiting for me in the den like vultures sharpening their claws.

"There she is," Mom gushes, in a voice that has the shrill edge of an opera singer off-key. She smiles in relief like she was afraid I was gonna make a run for the door rather than face this incredibly awkward situation she's put me in.

A syrupy smile drizzles over Kitty's lips. "Well, hello. Welcome home, sugar," she says grandly. Kitty is one of those country club women whose appearance and home look like a Pinterest post. Everything about her is disgustingly perfect in an *I'm better than you,* way. Collette looks fabulous as always with her long, platinum hair and even features. She's tall and as skinny as a rail. Normally, I would consider Collette's body size and type a blessing. After all, it's relatively simple to fit a dress to someone who has a near-perfect figure. However, since it's Collette we're talking about, I can't think of one good thing that could possibly come from this project.

I press a tight smile over my face, the one I've used many times when dealing with difficult customers. "Hello," I nod as I sit down in the nearest chair. I can feel Collette assessing me and have to fight the urge to scowl at her.

"Thank you so much for taking us on last minute," Kitty begins. "We had an appointment set up with Margaret Bradshaw, but she had to leave town suddenly when her sister passed away."

"That's terrible about Margaret's sister," I mumble. While I don't know Margaret super well, the town of Comfort is small enough that I know nearly everything about her. Her husband died a couple years prior, and her children are all grown and live in different states. At any rate, I feel sorry for her situation.

"Yes, it is," Kitty says absently like she couldn't care less. Her flippant attitude about another person's distress makes me dislike Kitty Williams even more. I can't for the life of me understand why Mom puts up with her drama.

Kitty purses her lips and adopts a piteous expression. "Your mother told me about the store closing and you losing your job. That must've been tough. You had such high hopes about conquering the world. You worked so hard and now here you are back home. I'm so sorry," she purrs.

Rather than answering, I pin Mom with a look that says, *Do you seriously expect me to work for these people?*

Mom shoots me an apologetic look as nervous laughter trembles from her lips. Then her voice takes on the edge of a knife blade as she turns to Kitty. "Albany is one of the most talented and determined people I know. Yes, it's been hard for her to come home, but I have no doubt that she'll land on her feet."

Wow. Go, Mom! I stifle a grin. Mom just put Kitty Williams in her place faster than the woman could blink. Maybe Mom has more fire in her belly than I thought.

"Of course," Kitty soothes as a cheery smile curves her lips. The smile is so wide that it probably would've filled her entire face had she not been injected with so much Botox. Kitty's face is so set that not even an earthquake could jiggle her features.

"Thanks," I murmur, surprised by Mom's compliment. It boosts my courage a little and prompts me to sit up taller in my seat. Will I land on my feet? I'll certainly try.

"If you're looking for a job, Collette can put in a good word for you at the bank. She's now the assistant manager," Kitty finishes with a note of pride.

I turn my attention to Collette and can tell from her smirk that I would be the last person she would ever put in a good word for. The two of us meet eyes. The grudge between us is as alive as it ever was—maybe even stronger than before. Except, this time, the tables are turned. Collette has the upper hand now because she's marrying Gavin. She enjoys seeing me so low and dejected. She knows what it'll cost me to alter her wedding dress. "If you work at the bank, then I'm surprised you're here … during working hours."

"It's my day off," Collette replies stiffly.

I don't have to look at Mom to know that she's giving me the evil eye. She hates it when I get confrontational. Rule number one of the Southern Belle's handbook states that a woman should never cause a scene. You can be as catty as you please, but you must keep a smile fixed firmly on your face and level your jabs with genteel civility. "Thanks for the offer," I say easily, "but I think I'll strike out on my own with the alterations." Yikes! Did I really say that? I don't want to do alterations, but I refuse to let Collette Williams and her snooty mother get the best of me.

This time, I dare to steal a glance at Mom. She gives me a look that says, *Cut out the shenanigans.* Mom's right. I'm acting juvenile. There's too much bad blood between me and Collette to behave in any other way. I'm finding it hard to believe that Collette would agree to have me alter her wedding dress, which makes me think that she's here to rub her engagement to Gavin in my face. Well, her evil plan is working. I'm so green with envy that I could make The Wicked Witch of the West look pale in comparison. Okay, time to stop wallowing in pity and get this show on the road. "What do you need done?" I motion to the garment bag draped over Collette's lap.

"I need the dress taken in," Collette sniffs.

Kitty chuckles. "You can't believe how hard it is to find a dress that's small enough to fit Collette." She cuts her eyes at me with a clear insinuation that I'm a blob of lard. Yeah, I get it. I've let myself go. I need to get back into shape, both physically and mentally.

An awkward silence passes, and I realize that everyone is waiting for me to speak.

"Sure, I can take the dress in," I respond evenly. "What's your time-frame? When's the wedding?" I hold my breath, waiting for the answer. I'd like to know when the door will officially close on any last chance I have with Gavin. I know it's silly for me to think in those terms because my chance with Gavin was gone a long time ago. He made sure of that when he broke up with me. Still, the knowledge hits me square between the eyes like a sledgehammer that my idiotic heart has been holding out hope that somehow the two of us might get back together.

Kitty and Collette look at one another. "As soon as possible," Kitty answers.

I've never wanted to be a mind reader more than I have at this very moment. What silent information just passed between Kitty and Collette? I sniff out the chink in their armor like a hound dog on the trail of a rabbit. "Have you not set a date?" Hope kindles in my breast. Maybe Gavin is stalling.

Color rushes to Collette's face. Her fair complexion makes her look like she's the spawn of a tomato. She clasps her hands in her lap. "We haven't set a date yet."

I make a face. "Really? Hmm ... that's interesting."

Rage ignites over Collette's perfect features. Her words come out in a hiss. "Just what do you mean by that?"

Victory swells in my chest. A-ha! Collette still rises easily to the bait. Evidently, she never learned the first rule of Southern Belle etiquette about not causing a scene. Mom starts blinking fast like she's about to pass out. "Albany," she cautions as she touches her hair. "That's enough."

"I asked you a question," Collette demands through clenched teeth.

If Collette wants an answer, then by golly she's gonna get it. Right here. And right now. My voice goes sugary sweet. "I only meant that

13

Gavin can be elusive. The fastest way to send him running for the hills is to try and pin him down." I know that from sad experience.

"I beg your pardon," Kitty inserts as she throws me a scalding glare before placing a reassuring hand over Collette's.

I shrug. "You wanted an answer, so I gave you one."

Kitty turns to Mom. "I thought you said that Albany has changed."

For a second, I can't believe my ears. Has my mother really thrown me under the bus? I take one look at her sheepish expression and know it's true. "Seriously? You told her that?" My voice rises, but I don't care. "As if there was something wrong with me before?" I rub a hand over my forehead, disgusted with the whole situation. "You know what? This isn't gonna work. You'll have to get someone else to alter the dress."

"There is no one else," Kitty protests, her voice fluttering with panic.

I rise to my feet, but Mom holds out her hand. "Albany, calm down." Her voice is firmer than the mattress at my New York apartment. "Sit back down, and let's discuss this like rational adults. Kitty and Collette need the dress altered. You need a job. Just tell them your price."

A hysterical giggle chokes my throat. "This is insane."

"How much will you charge?" Mom demands.

I do a quick mental calculation and then tack on twenty percent for the pain-in-the-neck fee. "Eight-hundred-and-seventy-five dollars."

Kitty's eyes bulge. "That's outrageous. Margaret was only charging us two-thirty-five."

I flash a tight smile. "Well, since you don't have a date set for the wedding, maybe you should just wait until Margaret returns, so she can do the alteration."

Mom gives me a pleading look. "Really? Is eight-hundred-and-seventy-five dollars the lowest you can go? Be reasonable."

It's not about the money. It's the principle of the situation. "Yep, that's it," I clip.

"When can you have it done?" Kitty asks.

Dang it! I was hoping the high price would be enough to make Kitty change her mind. Evidently not. The woman is as relentless as my mother ... maybe more so. "I would estimate two to three weeks, but I won't know for sure until Collette tries the dress on, so I can see what I'm dealing with."

"Okay," Kitty sighs resolutely. "Let's do it."

"Let's go downstairs to the workroom," Mom says.

It sounds so official to hear mom say *workroom* when referring to the combination exercise and craft room. Before I left for New York, I used the space as a workroom, but that was eons ago. The good news is that my old sewing machine is still down there. I guess I'll have to brush off the dust and hope the dinosaur still works. When we get to the basement, I motion to the bedroom located off to the side. "You can change in there."

"I'll help," Kitty says as she and Collette go into the bedroom.

The second they close the door, Mom whirls around. "What's the matter with you?" she seethes.

"I don't know what you mean," I snip as I lift my chin.

"I'm trying to help you, and you're throwing it in my face."

"Did you really think that I would be okay with doing the alterations on Collette Williams' dress?" I feel my face go flush. "She and I can't stand each other."

Mom raises an eyebrow. "This has nothing to do with an old grudge. You still have feelings for Gavin."

"That's ridiculous," I spit. "I couldn't care less what Gavin McAllister does." I jerk my thumb toward the door. "If he wants to marry that bird-brained twit, then so be it."

Mom shakes her head, a look of weariness settling over her. "I don't know what to do with you."

I can almost read Mom's mind. She thinks I'm an odd duck and wishes I was more like my childhood best friend Penelope Primrose, whom I used to tease about being practically perfect in every way. "It's not your job to fix everything!"

"Keep your voice down," Mom warns.

I take in a quick breath, fighting to keep my voice even. "You and I both know that this isn't gonna end well with Collette. She won't be pleased with my work, no matter what I do."

"Give her a chance to prove you wrong," Mom urges. "I think you may be happily surprised." She steels her jaw. "And for the record, you don't need Gavin McAllister. You're much better off without him."

I know how Mom's brain works. I can practically see the wheels turning in her head. She's trying to make me feel better about Gavin, take away the sting from him dumping me. "Yes," I say dully. "You're right."

The door opens, and Collette and Kitty emerge. My eyes pop when I see Collette's wedding dress. It's exquisite—a designer vintage style that probably cost more than I could make in a year doing alterations. Well, the dress would be exquisite if it weren't hanging on Collette. Kitty's right. Except for her boobs, Collette is a toothpick. I don't think I've ever been that skinny. Not even when I was twelve. For better or worse, my figure is curvy. It dings through my brain that Collette didn't have boobs in high school. She's always been straight as a board. I don't have to be a brainchild to know that she's had a boob job. From the looks of Collette's sculpted nose, I'd say she's also had a nose job. While there are things about my body that I'm not crazy about, I'm one hundred percent natural … right down to my well-endowed chest. And I have the larger arms and wider back to prove it. Women with naturally larger chests have the framework to hold them up.

Mom jumps into helpful mode. "I'll get the safety pins, the measuring tape, and a pad and pen for you to write down the measurements."

"Thanks," I say tonelessly. My heart aches. I'm disappointed with myself for feeling so dejected. Mom's right. I am better off without Gavin. I still can't believe he's marrying Collette. He used to poke fun at her in high school for being such a spoiled brat, saying that he wouldn't wish Collette Williams on his worst enemy. What the heck has happened to him? I guess I've been away for too long.

Mom returns a couple minutes later with the goods as I get to work, pinning the dress. For a few seconds, I forget that I'm working on Collette's dress as my love for the art of sewing takes centerstage. I'm so focused on my work that I don't even realize that Mom and Kitty have stepped off to the side, jabbering about the latest gossip surrounding members of the Lake Pine's Women's Club, leaving me and Collette alone.

"Gavin was so sweet with his proposal," Collette begins, interrupting my thoughts.

My insides freeze.

"He took me to Mobile to this quaint little Italian restaurant." Collette's voice has an annoying sing-song quality. I'm so used to the rapid clip of the New York accent that, to my ears, Collette sounds like she's acting out a poor attempt of Scarlett O'Hara on the stage. "He even paid a violin player to serenade us as he got down on one knee and popped the question."

I probably should remind Collette that it's not smart to poke the hornet's nest when the hornet in question is holding an open safety pin.

"I hope this isn't too awkward for you," Collette continues.

It's all I can do to force my voice to sound neutral. "What do you mean?"

Collette chuckles. "I know it was tough when Gavin broke up with you. It's good to see that you've moved on." Her voice brightens. "Who are you dating now? Mom said you were head over heels for some doctor, but then he dumped you and ran off to a third-world country. I'm so sorry," she coos. "It's interesting how things turn out. You were the queen of the crop back in high school. And now ..." She shrugs her angular shoulders. "Well, it's just interesting."

One little prick with the needle is all it would take. I look longingly at the satin fabric. Nope, I'd better not do it. I'm in enough hot water with Mom as it is. Still, it would be so satisfying to give Collette a jab with the pin. It would serve her right for gloating. Talk about kicking a girl when she's down. Collette is merciless.

"I can help you find a date if you'd like. It's the least I can do."

Did she really just say that? "Thanks," I hum, "but I'm good."

"Gavin's taking me to Maui on our honeymoon."

An invisible fist clutches my stomach. When Gavin and I were together, he promised that one day, he'd take me to Maui. It was something we dreamed about together. It became our imaginary place —the spot where everything would converge in perfection. I can't believe he's taking Collette there! It's the ultimate betrayal. Rage burns like a blowtorch through my veins. I move the pin into striking position. *Don't do it*, the angel on my shoulder urges. *What've you got to lose?* the devil on my other shoulder argues. I suspect that Collette knows that Maui was mine and Gavin's favorite daydream. That's why she insists on tormenting me about it.

"Did you hear what I said?" Collette prompts in the pompous tone of one who has the world by its tail. "Gavin's taking me to M— Mwwah!" she squeals when I jab the pin into her hip. I take it out as fast as the pin goes in.

Collette whirls around, enraged. "You did that on purpose." Her eyes bulge as she twists her head around to inspect the damage. The small red circle of blood on the white satin fabric is evidence of my dastardly deed.

Mom and Kitty rush over. "What's going on?" Kitty demands.

"She pricked me!" Collette wails. "Look, there's blood on my dress."

"Oops," I utter contritely. "My hand must've slipped."

"That's it!" Kitty seethes. "We are out of here!" She turns to Mom. "You're a good person and friend, Sable. Too bad I can't say the same about your horrible daughter." She shoots me a look so blistering that it's a wonder it doesn't cause the skin to peel right off my bones.

Mom's face is as pale as a statue. To the point where I almost feel sorry for her ... *almost*. Until I remind myself that this whole debacle is her fault.

"Let's go!" Kitty growls.

"But I need to get this thing off to get the blood out," Collette protests. "Otherwise, my dress'll be ruined."

"Run it under cold water," I suggest. "It'll do the trick every time."

Collette gets up in my face. Her words fly out in a hissy, saliva droplets splattering onto my skin. "You're a monster." She grunts. "You'll get what's coming to you soon enough."

I have no idea what Collette's talking about, and I don't wanna know. I'm so done with Collette Williams. I roll my eyes as I take a step back and wipe her disgusting spit off my face. "Good grief, I don't see what the big deal is. It was only a pinprick."

CHUNKY MONKEY

J need ice cream, and I need it now. I pull into the first open parking space I can find at the Piggly Wiggly. To say that Mom is ticked would be the understatement of the year. After Kitty and Collette stormed out of the house, Mom broke into a tirade of, *"Albany Jane Featherstone, I don't get you. You take everything I try and do for you and throw it back in my face."*

Therein lies the problem. For all her good qualities, my mom is selfish. She believes that everything revolves around her. I tried to explain that my beef with Collette has nothing to do with Mom, but she just doesn't get it. Then, when I thought things couldn't get worse, Mom announced that she'd set me up on a blind date for tomorrow night with some podiatrist from Mobile named Wallace Bogart the Third. "After the little stunt you just pulled, you owe me," Mom seethed before marching off and barricading herself in her bedroom.

That's when I decided to take a trip to the Piggly Wiggly and get some much-needed supplies … starting with ice cream. Lots of it!

The nerve of Mom setting me up with some podiatrist. Eww! The last thing I want to do is go out with some pretentious podiatrist. Also, what was Mom thinking with the alteration thing? She knows that I was heartbroken when Gavin broke up with me. How could

Mom have thought that I would alter Collette's dress? Maybe all of that hairspray that Mom insists on caking onto her hair has eaten through her scalp and destroyed her brain cells.

I grab a buggy and make a beeline to the frozen foods section. I pass a couple of people on the way. It doesn't register in my brain that they are smiling and nodding a greeting until I get past them. In New York, it's rude to make eye contact with strangers. Here, it's the norm. I'm sure the two people I passed think I'm a snob for ignoring them. I'll have to remember to be more congenial.

"Albany Jane, I heard you were back in town," a voice says from behind me.

Great! Just what I need right now ... to have to make small talk. Plastering a smile over my lips, I turn around.

"Hello," I say with genuine sincerity, relieved that the person standing in front of me is Fern Primrose, the mother of my former best friend Penelope, or Pen as she likes to be called. I guess I shouldn't say that Pen is my former best friend. That makes it sound like we had a falling out. We didn't. We just drifted apart as people do. I went to New York. Pen stayed in Comfort and ended up marrying Timothy Norwood, one of the darlings of the town. The Norwoods are the closest thing that we have to royalty in Comfort, Alabama. Their ancestors were one of the founding families. Timothy and Pen live in a mansion in the historical section of town that has been in Timothy's family for generations. My practically perfect friend finally got her practically perfect life—picket fence, neat rows of flowers, and all.

"How are you?" Fern asks.

An automatic reply blips from my lips. "Fine."

"I'm glad to hear it," Fern says with a smile.

It has been a long time since I've seen Fern. She's frailer than I remember, and her hair has gone completely gray. Actually, it's more of a snow-white color. It's attractive and suits her, I decide. Fern's face is lined, the edges of her eyes ruffled in deep wrinkles. She's around the same age as my mom, but she looks at least a decade older. In Fern's defense, she has fibromyalgia. Her health has always been tenuous, even back when I was in high school. She works as a librarian for the elementary school. Whenever I think of Fern, I picture her with a book in hand. Her husband left her for another woman when Pen and her older brother Beau were kids. To my knowledge, Fern has never dated or gotten involved with anyone else.

I've always liked Fern. She has an aura of contentment about her that few people ever find in this life. Fern strikes me as being happy with herself and her life. She's not one to constantly go searching for the pot of gold at the end of the rainbow, but rather has the rare perceptiveness to realize that the brilliance of the rainbow itself is the true gift.

Fern leaves her buggy and enfolds me in a hug. I catch a whiff of baby powder and something fruity, probably her shampoo. "I'm so glad you're back," she breathes.

"Thanks," I mumble, wishing I could say the same. When I was in New York, I was so sure of my place in the world. Now, I feel like someone has taken my life, shoved it in a blender, and turned the speed on high. And I'm supposed to make sense of whatever concoction comes out on the other side.

She gives me a searching look. "Have you seen Pen yet?"

"No."

Fern looks disappointed.

"It's been hectic since I've been home," I lie and then wince inwardly. Lightning is gonna strike me dead right here between the produce and deli sections of the Piggly Wiggly.

"You'll have to stop by." Her features tighten. "Pen could use a good friend right now."

My brows tug together. "Is everything okay?" It's uncanny how quickly my sympathies rise. Even after all this time, I still feel a sense of protectiveness over Pen.

"Yeah, she's good. She's settling into marriage and trying to make the Norwood Mansion her home." A wistful smile drifts over Fern's lips. "Pen is just wound up so tight. She needs to relax and look at the big picture rather than getting bogged down with all of the social drama. I tell her that she should take time for herself and start painting again." She pauses. "I wish Pen were more like you. More outspoken, more willing to follow her dreams."

I try to squelch the startled laughter that rises in my throat, but it escapes out as a half-squeak. "Me?" I don't feel like a success. I feel like I'm starting over at the bottom. A new revelation hits me, and I discover the root of the problem in my life—Pen and I have the wrong mothers. Had mine and Pen's birthdays not been two months apart, I would have sworn we were switched at the hospital. What my mother would give to have Practically Perfect Pen as her daughter instead of me. I guess pairing Pen and me with opposites was nature's way of evening out the playing field. "Thank you," I say to Fern, still trying to process her compliment.

A second later, I notice the expression on Fern's face. There's some sort of worry or secret behind Fern's eyes that lets me know that Pen is not okay. I run my mind through a list of possible problems—health, marriage, job, infertility. Surely Pen isn't considering having a baby. She and Timothy have been married for less than a year. They're still in the newlywed phase. I would think it would be tough enough to adjust to marriage without adding a baby into the mix. Then again, what do I know? I'm certainly no relationship expert. And, I'm dreadful at listening to the intuition of my inner voice. Ever since I came home, I've had the nagging feeling that I needed to go and see Pen. I just couldn't make myself do it, thinking it would be too hard to see Pen and her perfect life while mine is in shambles. Hot guilt blankets me. I should've listened to that inner voice and stopped being so selfish. I get so frustrated at Mom because she's so self-centered. I guess the apple doesn't fall far from the tree. I need to do better— whip myself into shape. I'm not this defeated girl that life has thrown for a loop. I'm a fighter, dad-gummit. I will fight … after I've had my ice cream and a long binge session of Netflix.

I talk to Fern for a few more minutes, during which time she makes me promise to go and visit Pen. I assure her that I'll go soon. Curiosity is now pricking at me, making me wonder what's wrong with Pen. Surely, if it were something devastating like cancer Fern would tell me. Maybe Pen is just down in the dumps. It happens to the best of us. She's probably trying to come back down to earth after marrying the man of her dreams. Pen has been enamored with Timothy Norwood ever since I can remember. Personally, I don't see what the big deal is. Timothy is too much of a pretty boy for my taste. I shouldn't generalize, but it has been my experience that guys born with silver spoons in their mouths end up becoming putzes. Okay, that's a bit of an overstatement. I guess time will tell if my theory applies to Timothy. I hope for Pen's sake that he'll beat the odds.

As I pass the meat department, a low wolf whistle stops me cold. What is it with meat departments? Ever since I was a teenager, the guys who work in the meat department get their jollies out of ogling all the girls. This would never happen in New York! Down here, it's everyday business. Although, no one has ever been brazen enough to whistle at me before. I turn and scowl. The guy behind the counter is sporting a goofy grin.

"Hey, Albany, welcome home."

It takes me a second to merge the image of the hunky guy with my memory. My jaw drops. "McKenzie Holder, is that you?"

He holds up his hands as a broad smile tips his lips. "In the flesh. It's Mac now, by the way."

The McKenzie I knew was scrawny and annoying with a whiny voice. Time has certainly done him good. I wheel my buggy closer to the counter so I can talk to him without yelling across the store.

He looks me up and down with a bold eye of appreciation that instantly gets on my nerves. "You look great."

"Thanks. So do you."

A low chuckle sounds in his throat, sounding like *heh, heh.* "That's what they tell me."

I fight the urge to laugh. McKenzie was always cocky. At least now he has the looks to back it up. He's well-built, and considering that his shirt is sleeveless, I'm getting a great view of his muscles. I'm sure that's the intent—for McKenzie, or Mac—to show off his body. He reminds me of the cartoon character Johnny Bravo. Sure, he's pleasant to look at, but he doesn't have much upstairs. I'm not just saying that because Mac works in the meat department. He was dense in high school, and I get the feeling that not much has changed.

"Hey, now that you're back, the least I can do is take you out for a beer."

He speaks as though taking me out would be doing me a favor. I moisten my lips. "Sorry, but I don't drink." It's bad enough for me to be so addicted to ice cream. No way am I gonna add drinking to that list. I like being in control of my own faculties. Also, liquor puts on the pounds. I'd rather eat my calories rather than drink them.

"I can live with that. We can get pizza instead. How about tomorrow night?"

It's on the tip of my tongue to say no, but then I remember the blind date with the podiatrist. I reach a fast decision. "I'll go." Mom's gonna blow a gasket when she realizes I'm going out with McKenzie Holder. The fiendish part of me takes a second to gloat over that fact. Maybe it'll teach Mom to stop interfering in my life.

"Rad," he bellows. "I'll pick you up at your place tomorrow."

"Sounds good."

"Nice blouse," he winks.

"Uh, thanks." At least he had the sense to call it a blouse rather than a shirt.

I can feel his eyes on me as I move away from the counter. Somehow, I get the feeling that I'm gonna regret my spur-of-the-moment decision to say yes to Mac Holder. His leering gaze tromps on my nerves. Oh, well. It's just one date. And maybe it'll get Mom off my back.

I make my way over to the ice cream section. To my dismay, there's not a single container of Chunky Monkey, my favorite Ben and Jerry's ice cream, left. The label is there, but the slat, shelf—or whatever that thing that holds the ice cream is called—is empty. "Seriously?" I grumble. "Don't they know how to keep things stocked in this town?" I'm so disappointed I could cry. My mouth waters thinking about the silky banana ice cream packed with chunks of fudge and walnuts. Briefly, I consider driving across town to the other grocery store in Comfort—the Stop and Save—to see if they have

Chunky Monkey. No, that would be too much of a pain. I guess I'll have to make do with the Peanut Butter World and Cookie Dough flavors instead. I pull open the freezer door and start chucking cartons into the buggy.

A low chuckle sounds behind me. "Still eating ice cream, I see."

I recognize the melodic voice instantly. It melts my insides to sloshing goo as I turn around. "Hey, Gavin." My eyes flick over him. Good grief, he looks good. Yeah, I'll admit it. I'm ogling. That'll teach me not to cast judgment on Mac Holder.

Gavin flashes me his trademark lopsided grin, the one that has been known to sweep me and half the female population of Comfort off their feet. "Your mom told me you were coming home. I figured I'd run into you sooner or later. How ya' doing?" He looks me up and down with an appreciative eye. Whereas I resented Mac scouring me with his eyes, I don't mind so much now that Gavin's doing it. My skin goes warm under his scrutiny, and I have to fight the urge to adjust my shirt ... ahem, blouse. "You look great," he murmurs.

My first reaction is that he's being sarcastic, but then I realize that he's serious. "Thanks." I'm part annoyed, part flattered, and mostly confused. If Gavin is so over-the-moon for Collette, then why's he looking at me with such open admiration? I never pegged Gavin as having a wandering eye. Then again, I never pegged him as ending up with Collette Williams either. I guess I've been wrong about a multitude of things. I feel like I've been blasted with a tropical heat wave. My body must have heated up ten degrees, and my heart is pumping like it's running a marathon. It's crazy the effect that Gavin has on me. A thousand memories slam through my mind in the flash of an instant. I see us huddled together at a bonfire the night before a big football game, the two of us sneaking into his neighbors' pool and taking midnight swims. We used to love to drive to the beach and play in the sand. We'd drive up to Ranger's lookoff point and recline in the back of his pickup truck, watching the stars and doing our fair share of kissing until the air would get heavy with the mist of the early morning. A wistful longing overtakes me. I feel so sad for all that we lost. I'm still ticked that Gavin broke up with me. I'm infuriated that he's marrying Collette.

His jade eyes zing with laughter as he points to the buggy. "No Chunky Monkey?"

Gavin was the one who got me into Chunky Monkey. "No," I lament, "it's out." It's then that I realize what Gavin is holding in his hand. My jaw drops. "Chunky Monkey? You got the last one? H— how?" I sputter. My brain tries to figure out what's happening here. Is it a coincidence that Gavin got the last container of Chunky Monkey, or did he somehow know I was going for it and beat me to the punch?

He shrugs. "You're not the only one who likes Chunky Monkey."

I straighten to my full height and pin him with a glare. "You got the last carton on purpose." I can tell from his sheepish grin that it's true. Did Gavin see me go into the store? Did he see me talking to Mac Holder? What would he think if he knew that I have a date with Mac tomorrow night? No, I can't go down this road! It doesn't matter what Gavin thinks because the two of us are through!

"I don't mind sharing. We can grab a couple of spoons from the deli."

My hand goes to my hip. "Don't you have to get back to the hardware store?"

A lopsided grin tugs at a corner of his lips. "I'm sure I can convince the boss to give me a few extra minutes for lunch."

My eyes move up to his messy hair. The last time I saw him, Gavin had cut it too short. Now, it's longer on top like I like it, giving him a boyish, reckless look. He's wearing a gray Panthers t-shirt, our high school mascot, and faded jeans. Gavin is lean with cut muscles. He looks more like an all-around athlete rather than a pump-you-up muscle monkey like Mac. "Ha ha. Very funny," I say dryly. Gavin owns the hardware store on Main Street and has the liberty to take as long as he pleases for lunch.

Adventure pings in his eyes, washing them in warm, mellow gold. "Whadaya say, Albany? You up for the challenge?" He pumps his eyebrows.

For a second, I forget that Gavin is engaged. I forget that he broke

27

my heart. All I can think is YES! I'm up for any challenge that concerns Gavin McAllister. Luckily, before I make an absolute idiot of myself, the rational side of my brain takes control. "What about Collette? I don't think she'd be happy about her fiancé sharing a pint of ice cream with his ex-girlfriend."

He blinks in surprise. "Who told you that I was engaged to Collette?"

"She did. About thirty minutes ago, when I was doing the alterations on her wedding dress."

His eyes round. "You're doing the alterations on Collette's wedding dress?"

"I was, until the pin I was holding had an unfortunate encounter with Collette's bony hip."

Startled laughter rises in his throat. "You jabbed Collette with a pin?"

"Yep, sure did." The corners of my lips twitch. Is it awful that it gives me a streak of satisfaction to admit that?

He shakes his head back and forth. "You always were a fireball."

Is that admiration I detect in his voice? Why does it give me such a swell of satisfaction?

"So, how about it? Let's go eat some ice cream and catch up."

The longing that I feel makes me angry. "I don't think so. What do you take me for?"

He frowns. "What're you talking about?"

"You're engaged to Collette," I remind him.

Amusement colors his features. "Since when do you care what Collette thinks?"

"I don't," I snap. "But you should care what she thinks, considering that you're marrying her."

Gavin tips his head and gives me a thoughtful look. "Are you jealous?"

My cheeks blaze hot. "Don't flatter yourself," I retort.

He grins. "You are."

I want to rip the smug expression off his handsome face. "You and I were over a long time ago," I growl.

He searches my face. "What did happen between us?"

I hate it when people ask a question that they already know the answer to. My anger rages to an inferno as I get up in his face. "How dare you ask me that? You know what happened! You gave up on us."

His face falls. "That's not how I remember it."

An incredulous laugh riddles my throat. "Is that right? How do you remember it?"

"We took some time apart so that you could go to New York and spread your wings. I was only trying to give you space so that you wouldn't have any regrets."

"Baloney! You broke up with me because you wanted the freedom to chase all the skirts you pleased." Gavin was at Jacksonville State University on a baseball scholarship. I knew that he had droves of girls throwing themselves at him. Him saying that he wanted to give me space was an excuse to sow his wild oats. Hurt bubbles up in my chest. I can feel a wall of tears pressing behind my eyes, but I'll be darned if I let a single one fall.

"No," he counters, "that's not what happened. I gave you space, and then you broke it off."

What he's saying is technically true. He wanted space, so I gave it to him. End of story.

My head feels like it's on fire. I glance around and realize that the older woman at the end of the aisle is staring. It's all I can do to keep my voice even as I hold out a hand. "Look, it doesn't matter what happened. The two of us were over a long time ago. It's ancient history."

He raises an eyebrow. "If that's so, then why's your face so red? Why're you so upset?"

"I'm not upset," I nearly shout, then swallow hard. Gavin has always been able to get my goat. One thing I like about him is that he doesn't mind calling my bluff. Of course, this time there's no bluff. He hurt me, and he's not gonna turn the situation around to pretend that he didn't. "I'm not doing this with you." I take a step back. "Who you choose to marry is your business," I mutter. "Just don't expect me to fix her dress."

"Speaking of clothes, that's an interesting shirt that you have on."

"Actually, it's a blouse." I lift my chin.

A grin tugs at his lips. "Okay, blouse. That's an interesting look with the bow thing that you've got going." His tone is teasing, taunting. "Is that some new style that you picked up in New York?" I look down and want to faint. My shirt has come unbuttoned across my boobs. Somehow—don't ask me how—the bow on my bra has managed to poke out of my blouse. The bow is positioned so perfectly that it looks like I've planned it that way. Humiliation scalds over me. I've been parading around the grocery store with the bow of my bra hanging out. No wonder Mac mentioned something about my blouse! He probably thought I was trying to solicit him. Oh, my gosh! What a day this is turning out to be!

"You're an idiot," I seethe to Gavin as I grab my buggy and flee the scene. I turn the corner to the next aisle and only pause long enough to button my blouse. No way can I face Gavin again. I hurry over to the canned goods aisle and go down it slowly, pretending to take interest in the items on the shelves. My hope is that Gavin will go straight to the checkout line, and I won't have to see him again. I wait a good fifteen minutes or more before meandering over to the checkout line. I would wait longer, but I don't want my ice cream to turn into soup. Gavin is nowhere in sight. Thank goodness!

"Looky, looky what the cat dragged in," Dimples Powell, the cashier, purrs with a broad grin as I step up to the register. "I heard you were back in town." Dimples is close to my mom's age. She's a pretty woman in a gaudy way with her big hair, hoop earrings, blue eyeshadow, and fire-engine red lipstick. "How ya doin', sugar?"

"Good. How are you?"

"Listen at that Northern accent. You've turned into a Yankee." She clucks her tongue. "I told Sable she was jinxing herself when she named you Albany. You've had New York in your blood from the time you were a young 'un. Sable should've taken a cue from me and named her daughter a Southern name."

I bite back a smile. "Like Dixie?" Dixie is Dimples' oldest daughter.

"Yeah," she laughs as she points a finger. "Now don't be sassing me."

"Yes, ma'am."

Dimples gives her gum a good go-around as she slides the first pint of ice cream over the scanner. Her acrylic fingernails are long and glossy red. I don't know how Dimples manages to work with them. Her head swings back and forth. "You've got some guts; I tell you that."

"What do you mean?"

"Honey, if I were fixing to parade around in a bathing suit on stage this weekend, I sure as heck wouldn't be loading up on all this ice cream."

I chuckle. "Yeah, me neither."

She gives me a funny look.

"What?"

Dimples leans close and lowers her voice. "Don't play dumb with me, missy. I know you're signed up to participate in the Miss Comfort Beauty Pageant this coming Saturday."

My throat closes, and I can't breathe. I make a gurgling sound to clear it. "There must be some mistake," I squeak. "I'm not gonna be in the pageant." I vaguely remember hearing something about the pageant, but I didn't think twice about it. Sure, I was a pageant girl once, but that was a lifetime and several pounds ago.

Dimples gives me a sly look. "You can act all innocent if you want, but Summer Heaton showed me the roster. Your name is front and center. You wanna know who else entered?" she whispers. Before I can utter a word, she answers her question. "Collette Williams. Summer told me that the only reason Collette signed up was because you're in it. She's been itching to beat you for years. After all, you're the only person who holds the honor of winning Miss Comfort two years in a row."

"That was a long time ago." My blood is thrashing like a washing machine against my temples. I know exactly how my name got on that roster … because my meddling mother put it there!

Dimples looks me up and down. "You're still as beautiful as ever with that long dark hair and those chocolate-brown eyes." She giggles. "Collette will be green with envy when she sees you. That poor girl is a carpenter's dream. Well, except for those ginormous boobs that she had installed." Laughter circles through her eyes. "Those things are so large that she could use them for floats. I'm surprised she's not having back issues. Yep, like I said, Collette will be jealous when she sees you."

"I doubt that," I fire back.

"Oh, she will," she laughs. "I guaran-darn-tee it." Her voice swings up. "Who knows. You might just win a third time." She tilts her head. "Although Strawberry Lingerfelt is on the roster too. Have you seen her lately?" She lets out a low whistle. "She's a looker with that red hair and those bright green eyes."

Strawberry is several years younger than me. The last time I saw her, she had her hair in braids, was covered in freckles, and wearing braces.

"I hope all this ice cream isn't for you," Dimples says as she puts the last pint into a bag and rings up my total. "You've gotta look great for this weekend."

"I'll be sure and share with Mom and Dad," I joke. I slip my card into the reader as Dimples jabbers a mile a minute. I hardly process a word she says. All I can think about is my mom. What am I going to do with her? I don't want the rest of my time spent at home to be a constant battle.

My mind is spinning like a kite caught in a hurricane as I drive home. As soon as I put the ice cream away, I charge into the den. Mom and Dad are sitting side-by-side on the sofa. Dad is dressed in his suit and tie. I stop in my tracks. "What're you doing home? I figured you'd be at the office."

He floats Mom a doting look. "I thought I'd take this pretty little thing to lunch."

Mom giggles like a schoolgirl as her face beams with pleasure.

Dad treats Mom like a queen and spoils her rotten. It's endearing and sickly sweet how in love the two of them are. Truthfully, I'm glad that my parents are still crazy about each other. I just don't feel the love right now because I'm so ticked at Mom.

"You wanna come with us?" Dad asks as he scoots forward and adjusts his tie. My dad is a big man who's all muscle. A linebacker in college, he's built like a refrigerator. His lively blue eyes are his best feature. I would kill to have eyes that color. Why did I have to get boring brown eyes like Mom? Dad's hair is going silver around the temples, giving him a distinguished look. He has a quicksilver quality that draws people to him. Also, there's an authenticity about Dad that lets people know they can trust him. His genuineness and keen wit are a winning combination, helping him build a successful law firm.

"No thanks." I laser in on Mom as my hand goes to my hip. "Why in the devil did you sign me up to participate in The Miss Comfort Beauty Pageant this weekend?"

Mom's face turns cherry red as a nervous laugh escapes her throat. Her hand goes up to smooth her hair. "It was a surprise. I thought you'd be pleased."

My voice goes shrill. "Pleased! This is a nightmare!"

"Hold your horses, butter bug," Dad cautions in an even tone. "Sit down, and let's talk about this."

I aim my wrath at him. "Did you know about this?"

"Yeah, your mother mentioned something about it, and I thought it was a good idea."

"Seriously?" I throw my hands in the air. "Y'all are both crazy!"

"Sit down," Dad says in a firm tone. "Once you hear the whole story, you might decide you wanna participate."

"That's not gonna happen," I spout.

"Come on, butter bug," Dad urges. "Sit down."

"Fine." I tromp over and sit down across from them. I fold my arms over my chest, glaring at them. I don't like how young and immature I feel right now. Yes, they're my parents, and I've been brought up to honor and respect them. However, I'm a grown woman with my own hopes and dreams. And I refuse to let my mother lead me around by the nose.

Dad turns to Mom. "Tell her about the prize money."

Mom straightens in her seat and moistens her lips. "Norwood Dental is one of the sponsors for the pageant this year. They're offering a ten-thousand-dollar prize to the winner."

My jaw hits the floor. "What? The years I won, I got a year's worth of free car washes and a coupon at Piggly Wiggly for thirty bucks," I mutter. There were a handful of other prizes, but they were all small things offered by local stores. Why in the heck is Norwood Dental putting up a ten-thousand-dollar prize? Now I really need to go and visit Pen. Her husband, Tim, runs the Norwood Dental Practice with his father.

"The pageant has come a long way since you were in it," Mom chimes. She shifts in her seat before crossing her legs and wrapping her hands around her knees. "I was thinking that you could use the prize money to open up an alterations' shop on Main Street. There's a spot opening up right next to the dance studio. Gavin owns it." She gives me a censuring look. "That's another reason why I was trying to get you in good with Collette Williams. In the hopes that Gavin would give you a good rate."

Laughter tickles my throat. "Well, that plan backfired."

Dad frowns. "What happened?"

Mom rolls her eyes. "Your daughter made a spectacle of herself today. I got her a job altering Collette's wedding dress, and she pricked Collette with a pin ... just for spite." Her eyes flash as she throws me a glare.

Dad's eyes widen the second before he bursts out laughing. His shoulders heave up and down. He laughs so hard that his face turns bright red and tears pool in his eyes before dribbling down his cheeks. Before long, I start laughing too. It feels good to break apart the tension inside me.

"Don't encourage her, Dallas," Mom blusters as she shoots me a dark look.

He shakes his head as he sucks in a breath and mops his eyes. "I'm sorry, hon, but you should've known better than to expect Albany to alter Collette's dress. You knew that wasn't gonna end well."

"That's what I said." Ten thousand dollars. The possibility rolls through my head. Hmm … I could use it to get reestablished in New York. Or I could open my own shop here in Comfort. Not alterations, but a dress shop. I could offer upscale brands, as well as a few of my original designs. Basically, I could take the plan for the store I was running and adopt it to Comfort. I can't believe I'm even considering this option. After all, how can I possibly stand living in a town where Gavin is married to Collette? Then again, it would give me the opportunity to be self-sufficient. There's no way I could start my own store in New York with ten thousand dollars. I don't even know if I can do it in Comfort for that amount. But at least it would be feasible here. I guess I'll have to give the idea more thought. At any rate, winning ten thousand dollars sounds pretty good, regardless of what I decide to do with it.

"What's going on in that little head of yours?" Dad asks.

I cock my head. "Maybe I will do the pageant." Even as I say the words, I wonder if I stand a chance. I wish I had a month to get ready. I could live off salads if I knew that I could win ten thousand dollars. No, I don't relish the idea of going up against Collette or any of the other girls. But I do have the advantage of having won twice before. Wait a minute. There's a dark cloud looming over this picture—Gavin McAllister. I can't stomach the idea of him being my landlord. Seeing him today unearthed all of the old emotions. "Are there any other open spaces in town … other than Gavin's spot?" Did I really just ask that? I guess I am considering opening my own shop. It's funny how quickly that idea took root. It would be nice to own a business. While I enjoyed working under Jeanine, my former boss and owner of the boutique in New York, it would be nice to be my own boss. To know that the buck stops with me. Do I have it in me to be a success? I would certainly like to try.

Dad gives me an astute look, and I swear he can read my mind. "Maybe it's about time that you and Gavin buried the hatchet."

"Not in this lifetime," I harrumph.

A sly smile slides over Dad's lips.

"What?" I demand.

"You're still carrying a torch for him."

My face flames. "Am not!" I nearly shout. Geez. Can I be any more transparent? I really need to develop a better poker face.

Mom lights up like a Mason jar filled with lightning bugs. "We'll need to get you a dress, shoes, and a swimsuit."

"I'm not sure how great I'll look in a swimsuit right now."

Mom studies me with a critical eye. "There are a few tricks of the trade that we can employ. Maybe some good shapers and butt-lifting tape for the swimsuit."

Dad cringes. "I didn't need to hear that."

"This is gonna be so much fun!" Mom squeals, bringing her hands together.

"Yeah," I say absently, my thoughts going back to the ten thousand dollars. For the first time since before the store in Manhattan closed, I feel a smidgen of hope. All I have to do is parade across the stage and smile and wave. I can do that ... I think.

Dad lumbers to his feet. "Let's go. I'm starving." He looks at me. "You coming?"

"Nah. I think I'll hang around here and munch on some lettuce." So much for the ice cream and binging on Netflix. I guess I'll have to go for a jog instead. There's not much hope of me transforming my body in a few days. However, I can at least try, maybe lose a little water weight.

This earns me an amused smile from Dad. "It's only for a few days, butter bug. Then we'll celebrate with a big bowl of ice cream."

"Amen," I boom.

As Mom stands, I hold up a finger. "Oh, I almost forgot. That date with the podiatrist won't work. Mom fixed me up on a blind date," I explain when I see Dad's puzzled expression.

He makes a face as he turns to Mom. "Sable, please tell me you didn't."

"She did," I insert, giving Mom a snarky look. It's nice to know that Dad's on my side.

He rubs his neck. "We've talked about this. I know you mean well, hon, but you've got to give our girl some space. You're smothering her."

"I had to do something to get her mind off Gavin McAllister," Mom mutters defensively.

Ouch. That stings. Yes, I'm a miserable sap. Why can't I just get over Gavin and put the past in the past? "I'm capable of getting my own date." I thrust out my chin. "In fact, I have a date for tomorrow night."

Mom looks suspicious. "You do?"

"Yep."

"With who?" she asks.

This is gonna be good. "With McKenzie Holder," I announce grandly.

The stricken look on Mom's face is comical. "Are you talking about Mac Holder, the meat counter guy at the Piggly Wiggly?"

It's all I can do to contain my smile. "Yep. He's the one."

"Have you lost your mind?" Mom hisses. "That guy's brains are scrambled. He ogles everything that wears a skirt. He was giving me the eye the other day."

Dad looks at me with concern. "As much as I hate to admit it, your mother's right. Mac Holder is a meathead."

Mom swats Dad's arm. "What do you mean 'as much as you hate to admit it'? What's wrong with agreeing with me?"

"Oh, hon," he soothes as he slides an arm around her waist. "Don't get all bent out of shape. I was saying that you were right."

Mom thrusts out her chin, fire flashing in her eyes. "You're darn tootin'."

I rise to my feet, planting myself in a battle stance. "I'm going out with Mac Holder." At this point, I don't care how big of a Casanova or meathead Mac Holder is. This has become a matter of principle. Battle lines are being drawn here, and I'm not budging an inch. I shoot my mother a death-glare. "I'm a grown woman and can make my own decisions."

"She's right," Dad cuts in before Mom can launch an argument. "We have to trust Albany's judgment."

"Thank you," I snip.

Mom looks like she's about to break into tears. "I just don't understand," she sighs.

"It'll be alright." Dad gives me a wink. "I'm sure Albany knows what she's doing."

Do I know what I'm doing? Going out with Mac Holder instead of the podiatrist had seemed like such a good idea earlier, but now I'm not so sure. At any rate, I'm committed, and there's no backing out. I just hope the date won't be a disaster.

Oh, well. It's just one night. If it's awkward, I'll have to grin and bear it. After all, what's the worst that could happen?

MY FACE IS UP HERE, MORON!

There's not much worse than going to a pizza place the caliber of Life by the Slice when you're watching your weight. The tender smell of baking dough tingles my senses. My stomach growls, hungry for all of the food that I shouldn't be eating. I can imagine the satisfying sensation of sinking my teeth into a pepperoni pizza piled high with cheese. Maybe I'll just have one teensy little slice with a salad. I'll eat it slowly, savoring every bite.

The conversation between Mac and me has been stilted and awkward, except when I give Mac free rein to talk about his favorite subject—himself. Mac is into wrestling and monster truck shows. I now know more about Bounty Hunter, Scarlett Bandit, Nitro Menace, and all the other superstar monster trucks than I ever cared to learn. Mac fits the part of a monster truck driver with his bleach-spotted denim shirt that's crudely cut out in the arms and the gold necklaces around his neck, one thick, the other thin. He has a diamond stud earring in one ear. Crikey! I feel underdressed in the jewelry department. All I'm wearing is a simple pair of gold hoop earrings. Mac must be super proud of his biceps because every few minutes, he casually flexes his arms when he moves as if to give me a show.

The worst part about this date is that Mac has a wandering eye. Every time a pretty girl walks by, he practically turns himself inside out to look at her. It's humiliating. I clear my throat to pull his attention away from the leggy brunette wearing a pencil skirt, clopping noisily on her heels, and toting a toddler. Mom's right. Mac doesn't discriminate. He ogles women of all ages, regardless of their marital status. Before the brunette caught his attention, there was the fifty-something-year-old blonde and then the teenager bounding past with her short, bobbed haircut. I should've insisted on meeting Mac here, so I would have my car. Then, I could just leave and save myself the pain and suffering.

I clear my throat to get Mac's attention. "What're you thinking of getting?"

He looks at me strangely, like I've asked something ridiculous. "A pizza." He reaches for his mug and takes a long swig of beer.

Watching him tickles my funny bone, causing me to snigger. I can't help but think of a comedy skit by Jeff Foxworthy where he drawls in a redneck tone. "I want a beer, and I wanna see something naked." Yep, that about sums up McKenzie Holder. "What kind of pizza?" I prompt. Do I really want to ride in a vehicle with Mac after he's downed a few beers? I guess I could eat crow and call Dad to come and get me. No, that won't work. He and Mom went to the country club to have dinner with Collette's parents, Bart and Kitty Williams. It irks me that my mom is so tight with Collette's mom. Where's the loyalty?

Mac interrupts my thoughts with three words, "Pepperoni and sausage." He speaks as though it's the only pizza on the planet.

"Sounds good. I'll have a slice of your pizza with a salad."

A goofy grin topples over Mac's lips. He leans forward, his eyes full of innuendo. "Hey, that was some blouse you were wearing yesterday." He makes a point of looking at my chest.

I bristle. "Excuse me?" I will not sit here and endure this humiliation. "My face is up here." *Moron*, I add silently.

He laughs easily as he pulls his eyes from my chest to my face. "How do you like being home?"

"It's okay."

The server approaches the table and takes our order. Just as she's sashaying away, it happens. Gavin strolls in through the door. My pulse increases as I swallow. I notice that he's alone. No Collette. As he passes by our table, he stops, surprise blitzing over his features. "Hey."

My response tumbles out of my mouth. "Hey." The dichotomy between Gavin and Mac is staggering. Gavin is dressed simply in a navy t-shirt and jeans. He looks tasteful, yet casual. He's the picture of class compared to Mac. My heart hurts. And all I can think is that I should be with Gavin.

Gavin looks at Mac and frowns before motioning with his finger. "What's this?" Gavin's disapproval broadcasts over his face as he looks at Mac. I can only imagine what Gavin must be thinking—that I've lost my mind or that I'm so desperate to go on a date that I'm out with Mac. Both of those assertions would be correct. I was an idiot to go out with Mac Holder. Dad was right. The guy's a meathead. We have absolutely nothing in common. I'd rather stuff pizza dough in my ears than listen to him drone on about wrestling or monster trucks.

Mac thrusts out his chest as he catches eyes with Gavin. "What does it look like, man? Me and my lady are out on a date." He throws me a cavalier smile.

I want to crawl under the table. "I'm not your lady," I sling back.

Mac's grin widens. "That'll soon be rectified once me and you get acquainted after dinner." He makes a point of staring at my chest.

I feel like a grimy piece of meat. "That does it," I hiss as I scoot back my chair and spring to my feet. "This date is over!" My face is burning like I'm standing two feet away from the sun.

"What's wrong, baby?" Mac asks with a shocked expression. The moron doesn't even have enough sense to realize what he did to offend me.

"I'm not your baby. And for the record, my face is up here!" I point to my face. "Not down here," I add, motioning to my chest.

I grab my purse and stalk out of the restaurant. I have no idea how I'll get home, but I'd rather figure that out than spend another minute with Mac Holder. The cool air feels good against my hot cheeks. Tears well in my eyes, but I blink them back. I steel my jaw, refusing to let myself cry. I guess I'll have to call Dad and interrupt his and Mom's dinner. They'll love that. I march down the sidewalk with the intent to get as far away from Mac Holder as I can.

"Albany!"

I pause, recognizing the voice. Everything in me wants to turn around, but what good will it do? Gavin is engaged to marry another woman. Not just any woman, but my childhood nemesis. I shake my head and keep walking.

"Hold up," Gavin says as he catches hold of my arm.

I stop, turning to face him. "What do you want?" I hurl through gritted teeth.

He holds up a hand. "Take it easy." He juts his thumb back toward the restaurant. "What was that about? Were you actually on a date with Mac?"

The incredulousness of his voice stomps on my last nerve. "Yes, I was," I state with all the confidence I can muster. "Is that a crime?"

Amusement swirls in Gavin's eyes. "Yes," he chuckled. "No woman should be put through that, especially not you."

What does he mean by that? I search his eyes. They're so green that I could get lost in the depths of them.

"How are you getting home?"

I shrug. "Walking, I guess." It's five miles from home. It'll take me a while, but I'll get there. I'd rather walk home than pull Dad away from his dinner. Mom would love nothing more than to rub it in my face that the date was a disaster. I don't think I'll give her the pleasure.

A lopsided smile tugs at his lips, making him look adorable. "In those shoes?"

"I can take them off and go barefoot. I'm a country girl."

He chuckles. "I knew she was in there somewhere. Let me give you a ride."

He has no idea how tempting it is to take him up on his offer. Do I dare? I straighten my spine, my eyes narrowing. "Where's Collette?"

"I'm not sure," he answers casually. "So, what will it be? Walking home barefoot or accepting a ride from an old friend?"

My insides stiffen. "Is that what we are? Old friends?"

His gaze locks with mine. "That and much more," he murmurs.

Ribbons of heat ripple through my stomach. It's sickening how attracted I am to Gavin. For me, it has always been him. I'm so painfully aware of that fact right now that it makes my head hurt. My eyes lock with his. Time seems to slow. I can feel my breath coming in uneven snatches, the blood pumping through my veins. There's so much I want to tell Gavin, like how much I still care. I've always cared. That's why I poured myself into my job so that I could fill the hole in my heart. I want to know why Gavin gave up on us. I want to know how he could marry Collette. How can he not care about me the way I do about him? I guess that's the painful aspect of love—the heart chooses who it wants, regardless of the circumstance.

I step back and shake my head. "Thanks for the offer," I say dully, "but I'm better off just walking home." I turn and walk away, my heeled sandals clipping out a fast cadence against the sidewalk. A very large part of me hopes that he'll call out to me or chase after me, but he doesn't. It's probably a good thing because if he did come after me, I don't know that I would have the strength to turn him away.

I walk past the shops on Main Street. It's not until I turn onto a side street that I allow the tears to fall. They flow freely down my face, and I don't bother wiping them away. It doesn't take long for my sandals to start digging into my feet, so I take them off and carry them in one hand. I'm sure I'm a spectacle. I don't have to look at the passing cars to know that everyone is staring. Before long, the side-walk will end, and I'll be forced to walk along the side of the road. For all of my bravado about being a country girl, the soles of my feet are tender. I don't relish walking along the gravel edge of the road. I guess I'll have to veer off the shoulder and onto the grass.

I jerk when a truck pulls alongside me. My heart skips a beat, thinking it's Gavin, but it's Mac. He rolls his window down, propping his elbow out. "This is crazy. Get in the truck."

"No thanks." I keep my gaze fixed into the distance.

"Come on, babe. Don't be like that. I was just playing around at the pizza joint."

I whirl around, my temper getting the best of me. "I'd rather face down a pack of wild dogs than get in the truck with you," I seethe. "You're a womanizing moron."

"Suit yourself," he sneers as he squeals off.

"Good riddance," I mutter.

I walk a few more paces before another truck pulls up beside me. What is it with this town and all the trucks? I turn, ready to tell the person that I don't need a ride, when I realize it's Gavin. My heart hammers in my chest.

He rolls down the window, a smile touching his lips. "Here's the way I see it. No self-respecting gentleman can turn his back on a woman walking home barefoot. So, either you let me give you a ride home, or I'll just follow along beside you in the truck. Your decision."

I hope that the wind has dried my tears so that Gavin won't realize I've been crying. "What's your endgame here?"

He frowns. "What do you mean?"

"You broke up with me, Gavin." My voice hitches as I continue. "You're engaged to Collette. Why are you suddenly so concerned about me?"

"I've always been concerned about you."

I grunt. "Well, you have a funny way of showing it."

A horn blares. I look behind Gavin and realize that vehicles are piling up behind him. "You're blocking traffic. You need to go on." How could I have ever thought that I could start a business and be in such close proximity to Gavin without being with him? It wouldn't work. It's too painful. I need to get my life figured out so that I can move on to other adventures, far away from Comfort, Alabama, and far away from Gavin.

He grits his jaw in determination. "I will ... as soon as you get in the truck." His expression turns pleading. "Please."

More horns blast. "Get out of the road," a man yells.

"Come on," Gavin urges.

I glance back at the vehicles. "Fine," I grumble as I climb into the truck.

I'M NOT THE KISS-
AND-RUN TYPE

$\mathcal{A}$ dense silence fills the space between us until Gavin chuckles. "What?" I demand, shifting to face him. My eyes trace the firm line of his jaw. Everything about Gavin is masculine. While Gavin never mentioned any desire to own a hardware store when we dated, I'm not surprised at his choice of a profession. Gavin always liked to tinker with cars and build things.

"I'm still trying to wrap my mind around the fact that you went out with Mac Holder."

"You and me both," I say dryly.

A chortle issues from his throat. "That was some get-up that he was wearing. I'm not sure if he was auditioning to be a gangbanger or if he was peddling jewelry."

My lips quiver as I try to hold back my laughter. It peals out of me in short bursts that shake my shoulders. Gavin could always make me laugh. The levity has the magical effect of dissolving the tension between us.

"So, how did you end up going out with Mac?" Gavin asks again.

I let out a long sigh. "Mom was trying to fix me up with a podiatrist from Mobile. I wasn't gonna have her ruling my life, so I opted to go out with Mac instead."

"Your stubbornness got you in a pickle," he surmises.

"Pretty much."

My stomach growls so loud that I feel like I have a tiger inside me. I clutch it, embarrassed.

"We'd better get you some food."

It dawns on me that Gavin had gone into the restaurant to get something to eat, but then he'd come after me. "I'm sure you're hungry too."

A grin stretches over his lips. "Starving. How does the drive-in sound? We can get a cheeseburger, cheesy fries, and strawberry milkshakes."

Gavin is listing my favorite things. "Sure," I say indifferently. Then something occurs to me. "Do you really want to be seen with me at the drive-in? That'll cause all sorts of rumors. I can see the headline of Nellie Kinsey's blog now, *Hardware store owner and fiancé of Collette Williams reconnects with his old flame over cheeseburgers and milkshakes.*"

"Don't forget the cheesy fries," Gavin adds.

I blink several times, not sure what to make of his response. "So, you're truly okay with going to the drive-in?"

He gives me a sidelong glance, his eyes sparkling with a challenge. "Are you worried?"

"Truth be told, yeah, I'm a little worried." I just got back into town and don't want to tarnish my reputation right off the bat, especially if I do decide to open a boutique. No, wait a minute, I culled that idea. Or maybe not. I don't know what I want to do. I'm a bundle of hopeless confusion.

"Where's the rebel I know and love?"

I nearly choke on my own saliva. Did he just say the word *love?* "For a man engaged, you don't seem overly concerned about Collette," I retort.

"You seem awfully concerned about her."

The comment raises my hackles. "I couldn't give a flying flip what Collette Williams thinks," I spout.

He doesn't skip a beat. "Good. We're going to the drive-in."

Yikes! My snake-fangled tongue has gotten me in a bind ... again!

Gavin knows me too well. He knows my weaknesses and how to work them for his benefit. He knows my instinct is to come out fighting—fake it till you make it.

He arches an eyebrow, his voice taking on the musical lilt of amusement. "Unless you're chicken."

Laughter circles my throat as I wag my finger. "Your goading might've worked when we were in junior high and you wanted me to skip chemistry to make out with you behind the gym, but not now."

"You know you want a big, fat, juicy cheeseburger and some cheesy fries," he urges.

I could eat ten cheeseburgers right now. My traitorous stomach growls again. "Okay," I relent. "But when the tongues start wagging about the two of us fanning an old flame, it's your own dang fault."

"I'm a big boy. I can handle it," he says as he makes a U-turn and drives us back toward town.

The cheeseburger is delectable, worth every calorie. I don't want to even think about the pageant this weekend or how I'll look in a swimsuit. I just want to eat and relax. I catch the interested glances from the people in the car next to us. I throw them an annoyed look, but they continue to stare. "Why's everybody in Comfort so nosy?" I complain.

Gavin drapes on a smile before offering a friendly nod and waves to the people in the car. "Those are the Armstrong's. Phil's a handyman. He's in and out of the hardware store a lot. That's his wife Marcia with him."

"Well, they're certainly getting an eyeful," I mutter. "This is when I start missing New York and how everyone minds their own business."

"Speaking of New York … are you here to stay, or are you going back?"

His question is asked lightly, but I can sense the gravity beneath his words. I shove the last fry into my mouth before placing the tray in the empty bag. "Do you really care if I go or stay?"

He blinks in surprise. "Of course, I care. I've always cared."

Anger explodes through me like a volcano erupting. "Would you stop?" I hiss.

His eyes narrow. "Stop what?"

"Stop acting like you care. When I know that's a bunch of malarky."

"Malarky, huh?" His eyes dance with laughter. "It's good to see you getting your Southern accent back."

The wounds inside me spill wide open, bleeding poison into my soul. "If you cared so much, then you wouldn't have ended it," I fume as I clasp my hands together to stop the trembling.

He places a hand over mine. I flinch, giving him a questioning look. His touch is as warm as it is thrilling. I can picture squiggles of lightning bolts zipping through my skin. My eyes seem to have a mind of their own as they drink in his chiseled features. Up close, I notice faint lines around the edges of his eyes. He has a dusting of freckles over his nose. They're so faint that I wouldn't have noticed had I not been so close. His freckles used to be more prominent. His brow is creased with a matureness that wasn't there before. Gavin has transformed from a boy to a man. This knowledge reminds me of the years that have passed—years when we were apart, living separate lives. Rolled into my attraction is a sense of loss. The hurt is so familiar that it's a part of me, imprinted into my DNA. Everything feels surreal. So many times I've dreamed of being with Gavin again, and now I'm here. My eyes move to his lips as my breath comes faster. Would his kisses still consume me as they did before? Being in Gavin's arms was a heaven that I never wanted to leave.

A partial smile touches his lips. "I've missed this. I've missed us."

"What're you saying?" I croak.

He chuckles. "Do I have to spell it out for you?" His hand moves to my cheek. His touch is tantalizing as he caresses my skin with the back of his index finger. I know I should put Gavin in his place. Tell him he's a two-timing louse for being here with me. And yet, I'm caught in his spell. Everything in me yearns for him. I want to feel his lips on mine. Gavin is my kryptonite. The ache to my soul.

He leans in closer. I feel his warm breath on my face. My cells are alive with anticipation as I part my lips. The instant before our lips touch, knuckles rap against the window. I jerk back, startled.

Gavin rolls down the window.

"Two strawberry shakes," the teenage boy says in a bored tone. Then recognition slashes over his face. "Hey, Gavin."

"Hey, Ben."

The guy frowns when he sees me in the truck. "Who's she?" he asks in an accusing tone.

"This is Albany," Gavin says easily.

I force a smile. "Hello."

Ben scowls, turning his attention back to Gavin. "Does my cousin know that you're out with her?"

Hot, slimy guilt covers me as my cheeks flame hotter than the asphalt in July. I'm a slimebucket! No, Gavin is the slimebucket for bringing me here and for making a play for me.

"How much do I owe you?" Gavin asks, ignoring Ben's question.

"Four thirty-five."

Gavin pulls out his wallet and hands Ben a ten-dollar bill. "Keep the change."

"Thanks," Ben says with a large grin as he takes the money and leaves.

Gavin hands me my strawberry shake and a straw. Fury is scorching such a hot trail through me that I wonder if I'll burst into a ball of flames. I yank the lid off the shake and slosh the ice cream onto Gavin.

He yelps as he draws back, holding his shake in the air. "What was that for?"

"For taking me here and making me care about you again!"

His eyes widen. "You care?"

"Was that your intent? To have me and Collette chasing after you?" I grit my teeth as I point a finger in his face. "Let's get one thing straight here, buddy. I refuse to be the other woman!"

He shakes his head in bewilderment. "I can't believe you dumped your shake on me." He looks down at his saturated clothes. The empty cup is resting in his lap.

"Give me that." I grab the shake and straw from his hand. I tear off the wrapper, toss it into the empty bag, plunk the straw through the hole in the lid, and began slurping on the milkshake. Yes, I'm drowning my sorrows in ice cream, but it tastes good.

"You are unbelievable." He opens the door of his truck and gets out as the empty shake cup falls to the ground. He wipes his hands down his t-shirt and jeans to remove the ice cream. "Hand me that empty food bag, will ya?"

I do as he requests. He leans over, picks up the empty shake cup, and throws it into the bag.

Meanwhile, I'm sucking down the milkshake with a vengeance, mostly because I can't believe that I actually threw strawberry ice cream all over Gavin. He leans in and grabs the unused napkins resting on the console, using them to wipe off his clothes. Luckily, the bulk of the ice cream got on Gavin rather than on the cloth seat of his truck. Still, there's a trickle of pink along the edge of the seat. He blots it with a napkin, tosses the napkin into the bag, and leaves it on the shelf underneath the metal menu screen before getting back into the truck.

He turns and gives me a blistering look. "You haven't changed one bit," he fumes.

"Well, you have," I fire back. "I never pegged you as a two-timer."

He swears under his breath. "I'm not."

"Huh?"

"I said I'm not," he growls.

I lower the shake to my lap. "What do you mean?" I ask carefully. A curious hope springs in my chest as I wait to hear what he's about to say.

"Give me that." He grabs the shake out of my hand and begins sucking on it.

"Hey," I protest. "That's mine."

He gives me a thin smile. "Actually, it's mine." He brings the straw to his lips and takes a long swallow. "Just as I thought."

"What?"

"It tastes much better than it feels."

I hiccup a choked laugh as he starts the truck and backs out. I look at his clothes, remorse stinging me with the venom of a thousand hornets. Questions are percolating in my brain. "What did you mean about not being a two-timer?" My voice sounds small in my own ears.

Rather than answering, he stares straight ahead, one hand on the steering wheel, the other hand holding the shake as he sucks the liquid through the straw.

"Fine," I grumble. "Don't answer me." I fold my arms over my chest and shift away from him to stare out the window.

Several minutes later, I'm surprised when he turns into his neighborhood. "Where are we going?"

"To my house. You didn't think I was gonna wear this for the rest of the night, did you?" He reaches for his garage door opener and clicks it as he pulls in.

My mouth goes dryer than a tub of cotton balls. It feels intensely intimate to be going into a garage with Gavin. Somehow, I manage to find my voice. "I guess I assumed that you would take me home, and that would be the end of it."

He turns off the engine and angles to face me. An enigmatic smile pushes over his lips. "Oh no, Featherstone, you're not getting off the hook that easily. You and I are gonna finish our conversation."

At a loss for words, I just shake my head. He gets out, comes around, and opens the door. His chivalry makes me feel even more guilty for the milkshake episode. A part of me wants to apologize, but then I remind myself that it's too soon for that. I need to hear Gavin's explanation first. If he is engaged to Collette, then throwing a milkshake on him was small potatoes in comparison to him making a move on me. He places his hand on the small of my back as he leads me up the steps that go to the kitchen.

Gavin's closeness is intoxicating. Our eyes meet, sending an inferno of heat whooshing through me. All rational thought flies out the window, and I can't resist the temptation any longer. I fling my arms around Gavin's neck and stand on my tiptoes as I pull his face down to mine. All I want is one kiss … for old time's sake. Then, I'll somehow summon the strength to let him go.

My lips nuzzle his with featherlight persuasion, swirling delicious sensations around my spine. His arms encircle my waist as he pulls me to him. I press my body against his wet shirt and jeans as my hands slide into his hair. Our lips meet in an explosion of fire as we kiss long and hard. I've wanted this for so long. The real thing is even better than the daydreams. He deepens the kiss, sending me soaring into euphoria. When we pull apart, we're both breathing hard.

Ever so slowly, a quirky grin tugs at his lips. "We've still got it," he brags.

I giggle in surprise. "That's all you can think to say right now?" I nestle my finger around a lock of his hair. "I've missed you." As soon as the words leave my mouth, I regret saying them. Hurt batters my insides. "You hurt me." I can feel tears coming on as I blink rapidly to stay them.

Regret simmers in his eyes, turning them to dull coins of mossy green. "I know."

I jerk, not sure if I heard him correctly. "You know?"

He nods.

"But you said at the grocery store that you wanted to give me space."

My back is resting against the kitchen counter. He cradles his arms around mine. "I got cold feet. I was scared. I forced your hand by claiming that I wanted to give you space, and you broke up with me." His haunted expression calls to the wounded part of me. This time, I can't stop tears from pooling in my eyes.

"I'm sorry that I hurt you," he says tenderly. "Losing you is the biggest mistake of my life."

His admission startles me. Is he really saying these words, or am I only imagining this whole scenario because I want him so badly? "What?" I shake my head. "Why didn't you come after me?"

He gives me a sad smile. "How could I? You were living your dream in New York. My home is here in Comfort. I could never ask you to give up your career for me."

"So, you were just gonna marry Collette?"

"I was never going to marry Collette."

My head begins to spin. "But she said y'all were engaged."

"Collette proposed to me, but I turned her down. It happened several weeks before you came home."

I'm happy, relieved, and outraged at the same time. "W—why didn't you tell me?" I sputter.

A cheeky grin fills his face. "And miss out on seeing you seething with jealousy? No way could I turn down that opportunity."

Laughter tickles my throat. "You are a menace. I wasn't jealous," I bluster.

"Oh, yes. You were jealous. I've got the remains of the strawberry shake to prove it."

"Okay, I was a little jealous," I admit and then scrunch my eyebrows. "I can't believe Collette put on that whole charade about the dress and you taking her to Maui on your honeymoon."

It's Gavin's turn to be surprised. "What? I never told Collette I'd take her to Maui. That's our spot."

"I know," I assert heartily. "Collette was goading me about Maui, digging in the knife, so I jabbed her with the pin."

"Well, it sounds like Collette got what she deserves."

"I still can't believe you dated her."

He heaves out a heavy sigh. "She's persistent, and I caved." His eyes search mine. "Now that you know the truth, where does that leave us? Will you stick around this time or head back to New York?"

A smile tips my lips, and I feel deliriously happy. "You know, I'm thinking about sticking around for a while. Maybe open a boutique. I heard through the grapevine that there might be a spot opening up beside the dance studio on Main Street. Would you happen to know the owner?"

His eyes sparkle with the zest of the stars as a broad grin fills his face. "I might know a guy."

"There's only one little kink in my plan."

Wariness settles over his features. "What's that?"

"I need to win the beauty pageant this weekend, so I can get the ten-thousand-dollar prize for seed money."

He gulps out a startled laugh. "Are you serious?"

"Yeah. Do you not think I have a chance?" I'm a little miffed by his reaction.

"Of course. You've already won it twice."

"I know. I'm hoping that works in my favor."

"If money's the issue, then don't worry about that. I can give you the ten thousand dollars."

I roll my eyes. "I'm not a charity case." It's good to know that Gavin is so successful. While I appreciate his offer, I need to do this on my own. Let's face it. If push came to shove, Dad would give me the money, but that's beside the point.

He laughs. "Down girl. I'm only trying to help."

"I know." I cup his jaw with my hand, stroking my thumb over his skin. "We've been apart for years, living separate lives. And just like that, you're willing to give me the money to start my business?"

He doesn't bat an eye. "Of course."

I'm dumbfounded. "We can't just pick right back up where we left off."

Laughter streaks through his eyes. "I beg to differ. Remember how you reacted when I asked you to the school dance in the seventh grade?"

"You approached me in the cafeteria ... embarrassed me in front of my friends. We were in junior high." I wrinkle my nose. "I was supposed to hate boys. I couldn't let any of my friends know that I had a huge crush on you."

"And what did you do?"

I roll my eyes. "You already know the answer."

"I know," he hums, "I just like hearing you say it."

"Fine," I huff. "I'll say it. I did the only thing I could to save face. I dumped my plate of spaghetti on you."

He gives me a checkmate smile, his eyes raining laughter. "Case in point." He steps back and motions to his clothes. "The more things change, the more they stay the same." He gives me an astute look. "I didn't see you throw beer on Mac, even when he was being a bozo."

Hmm ... Gavin's right. "No, because he wasn't worth the effort."

His eyes sparkle with amusement. "Glad to know I made the cut."

"You're always worth the effort," I chime. It's time to make amends. I make a face. "I'm sorry about the milkshake. If I'd known that you weren't engaged, I wouldn't have gotten so upset." I hold up a finger. "But you did bring that on yourself."

"I guess so," he laughs. "It was worth it to get you going. I had to know if you still cared."

"Well, now you know." I give him a playful shove in the chest and can't help but notice how cut his muscles are. It's on the tip of my tongue to tell him how amazing he looks, but I'd better not show all my cards on our first night back together. Are we back together? I sure hope so!

"I'm gonna go and change clothes, and then we can dig into that pint of Chunky Monkey."

My jaw drops. "You still have it."

"Of course. I was saving it for just the right occasion."

I give him a speculative look. "Tell me the truth, did you spot me in the grocery store and then make a beeline over to the ice cream section to grab the last pint of Chunky Monkey?"

He makes a zipping motion over his lips, his eyes popping with mischief.

"A-ha! You did!"

Mellow laughter floats from his throat. This is what I love—the banter that flows so effortlessly between us. Maybe we can pick back up where we left off. In many ways, we already are. That kiss was something.

"Okay, if we're having a confessional, I may have been walking by the pizza place, and I might've seen you sitting at the table with Mac."

His admission gives me great pleasure.

"I'm glad you saved me ... err, my feet from that long, dreadful walk home."

"I'm here for ya," he winks. A second later, he clucks his tongue. "You are something to be reckoned with. In the matter of a week, you stabbed Collette with a pin and showed everyone your latest fashion trend with the bow on the bra hanging out of your shirt."

My face flames. "That was an accident. My seatbelt must've unbuttoned my blouse."

He continues, "You entered a beauty pageant and got back together with your old boyfriend." He gives me an appraising look. "You certainly don't let any grass grow under your feet."

My eyes widen. "Are we back together?"

A crooked grin pulls at his lips. "You betcha." He pauses. "Unless you're one of those who likes to kiss and run."

A giggle rises in my throat. "That's just it. I've never been the type to kiss and run." My heart is so light right now that it feels like it could fly up to the heavens. I can hardly believe that Gavin and I are back together. "As for the beauty pageant, you can thank my meddling mother for signing me up."

"I wouldn't be too hard on your mother. After all, she's the reason we're back together."

My jaw drops a mile. "Huh?"

"It's true." He lets out a long breath. A few weeks ago, Sable came traipsing into the hardware store and announced that you were moving back home. She pinned me with one of her steely looks and said, "*Don't you think it's about time you stop dinking around and tell Albany how you feel about her?*"

"What?" I sputter. "Mom did that? H—how did she know how you feel about me?"

"That's what I asked. You know what she said?"

I shake my head.

Sable came back with, "*Because I've got eyes, that's why. You need to stop moping around and looking so down-in-the-mouth. Oh, and you need to stop dating all the wrong women and go after Albany.*"

"I told Sable that I would do just that if I thought you cared." He grins. "I might've said something about how ridiculously stubborn you are and that if I did make a play for you, you'd probably throw it right back in my face. Sable agreed and said not to worry about that, saying she'd take care of everything."

A disbelieving laugh rises in my throat. "Mom played me! She knew I would be ticked about altering Collette's wedding dress." My mind works to assemble the pieces. "Was Kitty Williams in on the charade? And Collette? I can't imagine that they would be."

"No, I don't think so. I'm sure that Collette and her mom dreamed up that scheme about the wedding dress to drive a wedge between you and me."

"Kitty and Collette thought they were playing me and using my mother to do it, but Mom was playing them." I shake my head in admiration, a grin stretching over my lips. "I haven't given my mom enough credit." I chuckle. "She's a crafty one. You just wait until I get home tonight."

"Wait a minute. Don't go home and call Sable out on the carpet. If you do, she'll know that I ratted her out."

"That's true." I think of something else. "If I play dumb, then I'll have the upper hand."

Gavin smiles in relief. "That's the ticket."

A wicked idea circles my brain. "I could pretend that my date with Mac went splendidly well. Mom'll croak."

Gavin's brow creases. "Nah, that's a terrible idea."

"Why?"

He gathers me into his arms. "Because the only person laying claim to you is me," he utters as his lips take mine.

THE BEAUTY PAGEANT

*T*he high school auditorium is packed to the brim. I stand off
to the side of the stage and look out over the sea of people.
I spot Gavin in the center, three rows back from the front. Dad is
sitting beside him. My stomach churns, and I feel like I need to puke.
Mom touches my arm. "Are you okay?"

"Why did I let you talk me into this? Why!" I growl, balling my
fists.

"Take it easy," Mom warns. "You've got this."

"I feel like a fat blob." I look down at my swimsuit, remembering
my nightmare about being naked by my locker. This is almost as bad. I
have to go out and parade in front of an auditorium full of people. No,
not just people. Even worse, people that I grew up with. People that I
know! Tears rush to my eyes. "Did you see how good Collette and
Strawberry Lingerfelt look in their swimsuits?" I whisper. They are
definitely the ones to beat.

Mom grabs my arm, her expression one of gritty determination.
"Those other girls only wished they had curves like you." She lifts her
chin, her eyes flashing fire. "Collette's got nothing on you." A pleased
smile curves her lips. "You got Gavin."

"Thanks to you."

Mom blinks in surprise.

I know I said I wasn't gonna call Mom on the carpet, but I can't resist the temptation. "I'm onto you. I know you used reverse psychology with the alterations thing." My voice goes syrupy. "You laid it on thick with all that drivel about how you just don't understand me."

"Of course, I understand you," Mom chuckles. "You're my daughter. I know you better than you know yourself."

Emotion wells in my chest. "Thanks for the nudge. I guess I needed it more than I realized." I give her a tender smile. "You're alright."

Moisture fills her eyes. "You're alright too." Her voice hitches. "I love you."

"I love you too." My mom and I look at one another with a new understanding. It occurs to me that maybe I do have the right mother for me, after all.

Out of the corner of my eye, I catch sight of the emcee striding out on stage to begin the pageant.

"You've got this," Mom assures me. "Go out there and show 'em what Albany Jane Featherstone's made of. I would tell you to make me proud, but it's too late for that ... I'm already proud."

This time, I'm the one whose eyes go moist. "Thanks."

The music starts, and I see the contestants lining up. I straighten my spine and suck in my stomach. "It's showtime," I say mostly to myself as I drape on my beauty pageant smile.

An hour later, my feet are killing me in these heels, and I feel like my mouth is about to crack off my face from smiling so much. I have to keep reminding myself to maintain good posture, even though a dart of pain is shooting between my shoulder blades. I'm fortunate to have made it into the top three finalists. No surprise, I'm in the lineup with Collette and Strawberry Lingerfelt. Swarms of butterflies circle my stomach as I wait for the emcee to announce the winner. The ten-thousand-dollar prize has never felt so close or so far away. I look out into the crowd as Gavin catches my eye. The look of adoration on his handsome face makes my heart swell. He grins and gives me a thumbs up. Regardless of what happens on this stage, I realize with a jolt that I've already won the greatest prize of all—a chance to start over with the man of my dreams.

The emcee clears his throat. "The second runner-up is Albany Jane Featherstone." I feel a whoosh of disappointment as I hitch up my smile and glide across the stage to accept the bundle of roses and crown that are presented to me. I didn't win the ten thousand dollars. Now what? I guess I'll have to come up with an alternate plan.

"The first runner-up is Collette Williams," the host booms. "And the winner is Strawberry Lingerfelt."

As Strawberry is crowned and takes her walk across the stage, crying and waving at the audience, Collette shoots me a smug look. "I guess I won this round."

"Actually, Strawberry won," I point out. "But when it comes to what truly matters, I'm the real winner." I make a point of looking out at the audience and catching eyes with Gavin. I can almost feel the steam coming out of Collette's ears. I feel a little guilty for the jab ... just a smidgen guilty.

After the pageant is over, Mom approaches me, fuming. "This is all Nellie Kinsey's fault. If it weren't for her stupid blog and all that talk about you being a relationship wrecker, I know the judges would've picked you."

"Spoken like a true mother," I laugh. Maybe what Mom says is true. Maybe not. Strawberry Lingerfelt is a beauty with her mane of red hair and perfect figure. I feel like I came out okay taking third place, especially considering my lack of preparation. "I guess I'll have to come up with a new plan since I didn't win the prize money."

Mom's eyes light up. "No need for that. I've already come up with an alternate plan."

Uh, oh. There's no telling what Mom has up her sleeve. I'm almost afraid to ask. "What is it?"

A bright smile overtakes her face. "You and I are gonna open up a boutique together ... as partners."

My eyes bug. "What?" I shake my head. "Um, I don't see how that would work. The two of us would kill each other."

"Nah, we'll be fine," Mom chuckles. "The way I see it is that you have a great eye for clothing styles and design, but you're a bit of a blunt instrument when it comes to dealing with people. You need me to buff out the rough edges. I know how to navigate the Kitty Williams of the town." Her eyes sparkle. "Also, think of the business I can send our way as President of the Lake Pines Women's Club."

"I'll think about it," I say, knowing that Mom will eventually talk me into it.

After I change clothes and gather my things, Gavin and Dad meet us outside in the parking lot.

"You did great," Gavin says as he enfolds me in a hug and kisses me on the lips.

"Thank you," I breathe, relieved that the pageant is over.

"I especially liked the swimsuit part," he murmurs. "You looked like a million bucks."

My insides go soft as I smile. My phone buzzes.

"You'd better answer that," Mom says. "It's been buzzing like crazy for the past hour. Someone's desperate to get in touch with you."

I pull it from my purse. It's Jeanine, my former boss. "Hello," I answer.

"Finally!" Jeanine exclaims. "I've been trying to reach you for hours."

"What's up?"

"You're not going to believe this," she squeals, "but I just got funding by some new investors to open a store in Manhattan. I want you to come back and run it for me." My mind spins as I look at Gavin, Mom, and Dad. All three of them are watching me.

"That's good news," I say to Jeanine.

"Good? It's great! We're in the driver's seat. These new investors are in it for the long haul. They love what we did with the other store and want us to create the same model."

"I'm kind of in the middle of something," I hedge. "Can I call you back later?"

There's a slight pause. "Sure. You will take the job, right? I can't do it without you."

"I'll certainly give it some thought," I say neutrally as I end the call.

Gavin gives me a searching look. "Give what some thought?"

Dad touches my arm. "What's going on, butter bug?"

"Jeanine got funding to open a new store in Manhattan. She wants me to run it." I look at Gavin and see the distress on his face. His jaw tenses as his features go stone hard.

"What're you gonna do?" he asks.

A dry laugh leaves my throat. "I don't know," I answer. "This is so unexpected."

Gavin gives me a long look. "I guess that's that," he mutters as he shakes his head and stalks away.

"Are you just gonna let him walk away?" Mom asks, frustration simmering in her voice.

I rub my hand across my forehead. "I don't know," I say as I turn to look at Gavin. My eyes trace the outline of his defiant shoulders. I can tell from his stiff gait that he's wounded, angry. The feeling of loss that sweeps over me is a relentless tidal wave that's determined to pull me under. "Look at him," I bluster, "storming off like an idiot and not even giving me a chance to process my thoughts."

Dad puts a hand on my shoulder, offering me a tender smile. "Butter bug, what're you doing? You and I both know that no store is worth losing the love of your life. Go after him."

Just like that, everything becomes clear. "It's time to stop chasing the pot of gold at the end of the rainbow and start appreciating the beauty of the rainbow itself."

"Huh?" Dad asks dubiously.

"Never mind. No time to explain." I take off sprinting. "Gavin McAllister," I yell.

He stops and turns around. "Yeah?" he sulks.

A smile plays over my lips. "You getting cold feet already?"

He grunts. "Not hardly. You're the one who's kissing and running."

I bridge the distance between us and throw my arms around his neck. "You are the most frustrating man I know."

Amusement lights his eyes. "Does this mean that you're staying?"

His expression is as hopeful as it is vulnerable. I realize just how much Gavin cares, and it warms me to the center.

I square my jaw. "You'd better believe I'm staying. It's like I told you before, I'm not the kiss and run type."

A low chuckle rumbles in his throat as his arms encircle my waist. "Good to know," he murmurs as he captures my lips with his.

Coming home has never felt so right.

THANKS FOR READING COLD FEET. Read Penelope's story in Practically Perfect.

Penelope had her practically perfect life planned to the letter, but she never counted on him ...

OTHER BOOKS BY JENNIFER YOUNGBLOOD

Check out Jennifer's Amazon Page

The Honeysuckle Island Series

Chasing Whispers

The Fragile Truth

The Secrets We Treasure

False Illusions

To Steal A Heart

Good Girls Don't Come Last (Romcom)

Cold Feet

Practically Perfect

High Heels and Big Deals

Romeo Family Romance

One Perfect Day

One Way Home

One Little Switch

One Tiny Lie

One Big Mistake

One Southern Cowboy

One Singing Bachelorette

One Fake Fiancé

One Silent Night
One Kick Wonder
One More Chance

Billionaire Boss Romance

Her Blue Collar Boss
Her Lost Chance Boss

Georgia Patriots Romance

The Hot Headed Patriot
The Twelfth Hour Patriot
The Unstoppable Patriot
The Exiled Patriot

O'Brien Family Romance

The Impossible Groom (Chas O'Brien)
The Twelfth Hour Patriot (McKenna O'Brien)
The Stormy Warrior (Caden O'Brien and Tess Eisenhart)

Christmas

Rewriting Christmas (A Novella)
Yours By Christmas (Park City Firefighter Romance)
Her Crazy Rich Fake Fiancé
Her Christmas Wedding Fake Fiancé

Navy SEAL Romance

The Resolved Warrior
The Reckless Warrior
The Diehard Warrior
The Stormy Warrior

The Jane Austen Pact

Seeking Mr. Perfect

Texas Titan Romances

The Hometown Groom
The Persistent Groom
The Ghost Groom
The Jilted Billionaire Groom
The Impossible Groom

Hawaii Billionaire Series

Love Him or Lose Him

Love on the Rocks

Love on the Rebound

Love at the Ocean Breeze

Love Changes Everything

Loving the Movie Star

Love Under Fire (A Companion book to the Hawaii Billionaire Series)

Kisses and Commitment Series

How to See With Your Heart

Angel Matchmaker Series

Kisses Over Candlelight

The Cowboy and the Billionaire's Daughter

Romantic Thrillers

False Identity

False Trust

Promise Me Love

Burned

Contemporary Romance

Beastly Charm

Fairytale Retellings (The Grimm Laws Series)

Banish My Heart **(This book is FREE)**

The Magic in Me

Under Your Spell

A Love So True

Southern Romance

Livin' in High Cotton

Recipe for Love

The Secret Song of the Ditch Lilies

Short Stories

The Southern Fried Fix

Falling for the Doc Series (Co-authored with Craig Depew, MD)

Cooking with the Doc

Dancing with the Doc

Cruising with the Doc

Jackson Hole Firefighter Romance Series

Saving the Billionaire's Daughter
Saving His Heart (Co-authored with Agnes Canestri)
Saving Grace (Co-authored with Amelia C. Adams)
Saving the Rookie (Co-authored with Stephanie Fowers)
Saving the Captain (Co-authored with Jewel Allen)
Saving Forever (Co-authored with Shanna Delaney)
The St. Claire Sisters Series
Meet Me in London (Co-authored with Haley Hopkins)
Collections
A Merry Christmas Romance Collection
A Christmas to Remember Romance Collection
The Christmas Bliss Romance Collection
Christmas Romance Collection
The Cozy Fire Collection
Sweet Beginnings Series Starter Collection
Jennifer's Military Romance Collection
The Heart and Soul Collection
Texas Titan Romance Collection
Hawaii Billionaire Romance Collection
The Southern Romance Collection
The Romance Suspense Collection
The Originals Collection
The Spring Dream Collection
Forever Yours Collection

ABOUT JENNIFER YOUNGBLOOD

Jennifer loves reading and writing clean romance. She believes that happily ever after is not just for stories. Jennifer enjoys interior design, rollerblading, clogging, jogging, and chocolate. In Jennifer's opinion there are few ills that can't be solved with a warm brownie and scoop of vanilla-bean ice cream.

Jennifer grew up in rural Alabama and loved living in a town where "everybody knows everybody." Her love for writing began as a young teenager when she wrote stories for her high school English teacher to critique.

Jennifer has a BA in English and Social Sciences from Brigham Young University Hawaii where she served as Miss BYU Hawaii. Before becoming an author, she worked as the owner and editor of a monthly newspaper named *The Senior Times*.

She now lives in the Rocky Mountains with her family and spends her time writing and doing all of the wonderful things that make up the life of a busy wife and mother.

Made in the USA
Las Vegas, NV
14 June 2023

73383899R00046